Instant Fires

INSTANT FIRES
First published in 2022 by
New Island Books
Glenshesk House
10 Richview Office Park
Clonskeagh
Dublin D14 V8C4
Republic of Ireland
www.newisland.ie

Print ISBN: 978-1-84840-836-4
eBook ISBN: 978-1-84840-837-1

British Library Cataloguing in Publication Data. A CIP catalogue record for this book is available from the British Library.

Set in 12 on 16 pt Espinosa Nova Pro

Typeset by JVR Creative India
Edited by Neil Burkey, neilburkey.com
Cover design by Holly Ovenden, hollyovenden.com
Printed by Scandbook, scandbook.com

New Island received financial assistance from The Arts Council (An Chomhairle Ealaíon, Dublin, Ireland

New Island Books is a member of Publishing Ireland

10 9 8 7 6 5 4 3 2 1

Instant Fires

Andrew Meehan

NEW ISLAND

For my liebling

PART ONE

—

WINE WITH LUNCH

—

PART TWO

The people I grew up with were afraid
They were alone too long in waiting-rooms,
In dispensaries and in offices whose functions
They did not understand.

—'The People I Grew Up With Were Afraid',
Mickey Gorman

Now therefore, while the youthful hue
Sits on thy skin like morning dew,
And while thy willing soul transpires
At every pore with instant fires,
Now let us sport us while we may,
And now, like amorous birds of prey,
Rather at once our time devour
Than languish in his slow-chapped power.

—'To His Coy Mistress',
Andrew Marvell

PART ONE

9th of July, 2014

Summer was a long stretch and he would never reach the end of it. Dawn was the hour of his optimism dissolving, a great mischief of the heart to call his own.

He drove by the river, disdain off the geese. Up the town, disdain off the slates. The bells tolling the hour, and the sad surprise of four notes and more cooling of the jets.

What would it mean to be useful and do no wrong?

To Marktplatz, and the town's fountain pouring a portion of his soul. He was grateful for the tickle of a breeze, waiting it out 'til morning, admiring all the while the poetical notion of an ashen sky at dawn. An hour on the bench by the Rathaus, catching the tail of his favourite dream: a line-shaft a mile long powering the Holy Mountain. Soul drift.

A trellis of roses, the forest floor, just a whiff of it, and a heartleap at the sight of a haystack lonely in a field. His soul running smoothly as a loom.

They were unmistakeably in the middle of Europe. She had forgotten that a country of slow-moving rivers and brown forests could be so radiant.

On her way home to hide—Heidelberg was itself in hiding and on the way to nowhere in particular—she felt herself undercover, as well as completely overwhelmed by the sight of all the allotments and smallholdings just as she remembered them. The round-shouldered barns under which huddled saintly woodpiles, no movement in the long, limp grass, a haze upon all that sweet-looking lettuce.

No wind and little commotion to speak of made them a very docile people.

All the better that her first fleeting glimpse of the Neckar came by surprise. A view of the old bridge, rinsed clean and smartened up since the last time she'd seen it. The river shimmered and the tour groups gathered and in that regard her hometown was exactly as she expected it would be, only with more phone shops, and Japanese tourists coming from all directions; Indians, an extended family—mothers, sons, grandfathers, more—using the riverbank as a cricket oval.

The hills above the Philosophers' Walk were their usual bluish-green, but she was overawed by the sight of all those quietly powerful new buildings, and the way they had taken possession of the hill. One thing that hadn't changed was the Sankt Hedwig, an old tugboat on the Neckar that was now a restaurant owned by her parents' friends, the Völker-Steins. Maybe they would all run into each other at some point?

The day was warm and the altstadt was full of people.

As much as she had been keeping it alive in her mind, Ute had some trouble finding her way to her old door. The Pfeiffers' house on Bauamtsgaße overlooked an impressive cobbled courtyard off a lane off a hallowed street ruminating toward Heidelberg's famous river. She passed the building a couple of times before remembering that the workshop had been closed up. Oh mercy, the yard her mother used to populate with chives and bay and peony trees was lifeless with broken brushes and upturned bins and in all probability hadn't been swept all year.

There was a crack like the beginning of fireworks. The driver of a ship-sized BMW was attempting to make a turn in front of her parents' front door. Rather than turning, the car was moving back and forth, as though mowing a lawn. It would have been easier somehow to unpack the cobbles and move the courtyard than to get the car out of there without seventeen attempts to turn it around. The driver might have been about to plough into the wall altogether. No, he hadn't, yes, he had driven over some kind of a chicken coop. It might have been the stupidest thing she'd ever seen.

A young man in an old suit—a wool suit—stepped out of the car with all the assurance of someone who'd just screwed up their first driving lesson.

—Didn't you hear? she said. Didn't you see?

—I do now, he said. Sometimes he gets out for a nosey.

He got the hen up into his arms. On he went in a voice as tuneful as a chorister's, as though nearly decapitating the hen then singing to it was part of a daily ritual. The hen's eyes were speaking of longing, and worse than the smell was the bird snuggling. The noise plaintive and melodious.

—Thought its days were numbered.

—Whose hen is it? she said.

He made a move for the shadow, out of the way of her question. It wasn't easy at all to tell from where he came. He sounded Irish, he wasn't from Heidelberg, anyway. Germans had a veneer to them, which he was lacking. It had taken her some time—until now?—to realise what this look meant. It meant he was amused. Irish faces were so unreliable. Hours and hours of conversation and you wouldn't know one thing about that person.

—Is it yours? she said.

—My girlfriend's. My ex-girlfriend's. It's fine, it's someone's hen.

—It doesn't look fine. Are you sure it's okay?

—This is not a happy hen.

—Does it need anything?

—A bit of quiet.

The top of his head was pink with sun, bones breaking the smooth surface of his skull. He was clean-shaven yet below the ears and the hairline his neck and his throat and the tops of his hands were thick with the brick-coloured hair of a red setter. He was in that regard like a big, bald rescue dog, and hairy in the way that carpets in Nordic crime dramas were hairy. It would be like being made love to by a fur coat.

—What part of Ireland are you from?

—Wild guess? he said.

—I lived there, you see. Some different parts of Dublin.

—Up to here with our messing then.

—Not really. I like it.

—What had you there?

—I was with someone. Fifteen years, approximately. A long time.

—A long time is right, but glad to hear you weren't on your own.

—I wonder why I was ever there.

—Same as that, he said. You're here now.

He was panting as he packed the hen away in its coop. Nervous, she supposed. It suited him, and he was very unobservant if he couldn't tell that she was smiling to herself. Already it had a lot to do with him not being Tort.

That morning, as per their routine, she had heard him being quiet in the bathroom. No sooner had they returned from their most recent trip—he had boarded the plane in Tokyo with a conveyer-belt's worth of airport sushi—than Tort comforted himself against the doldrums of summer by planning the conversion of the bathroom at home into a private sentō spa.

He meant well and she knew that, but it was always best to ignore any of his more inane ideas. The most opulent part of the spa was not the enormous wooden bath with deep sides but half a volleyball court's worth of marble shining like fresh lamb fat. Today he had his bath and did the most spiteful of poos before leaving the house, perhaps for a meeting or perhaps for good, as she had done.

The Hide, his self-declared masterpiece, was two expensive boxes, one high-technology ice-cream wafer balancing on top of another. He had taken pride in being able to draw the plans on a cocktail napkin and, quite as easily as clearing his throat, had bought an entire caravan park on the coast in Wicklow—disposing of seventy mobile homes—so they could have access to their own private beach and nine-hole golf course. He had seen it as a project of obvious importance, like all the others, but faltered the first time he saw the structure loom against a sullen November sky. Overnight he acquired a new and indistinct taste in art tacitly explained by the size of the walls. Tort's eye had been formed in the lobbies of investment banks and hotels. A grand piano, and an enormous photograph of the murky sea by which they were already surrounded, were selected for scale rather than sensibility. The floor-to-ceiling glass suggested the imminent arrival of car salesmen. Some bookshelves, cunningly installed, were only accessible by a sliding ladder on the wall.

The ladder to heaven, Tort called it. The unreachable ladder to heaven.

Mama descended the stairs and walked unsteadily across the cobbles towards the river and town. The empty shopping trolley she was wheeling was causing her some concern. This seemed to be an ongoing difficulty and she didn't seem to notice Ute at all.

Then, over her shoulder, —It's you.

—Hello, Mama.

—You've done something to yourself.

Many people considered giving yourself a haircut a strange thing to do, but Ute thought letting a stranger near you with scissors to be just as peculiar. She'd been doing the same thing for years anyway, the only problem being the fineness of her hair. It was so flyaway. Just when you thought everything had been gathered up, you found that some hair had made its way out of the bathroom onto your pillow or even into the milk. Blonde clouds everywhere.

—Are you going anywhere special?

—I had thought so.

—That style is something you do for a special occasion.

In the end, Ute had decided upon the trip at the last minute. What she had packed was hardly enough to cover a long weekend in the country. She should have been better at preparing for trips by now.

—You look well, Mama, Ute said, even though she didn't.

Her chin was going, and there were shadows in the folds of skin on her neck. Ute saw how her mother wore her hair now, roughly shorn like a summer ewe.

—I was on my way out, Mama said.

Papa was under the weather, she said. He couldn't bear surprise visits. Ute would have to make do with yesterday's bread. There was no hand towel in the bathroom. The bathroom had been redone anyway, and Ute wouldn't like it. The recycling was cluttering up the hallway. Her mother covered every single reason why Ute was not welcome in her own home.

In summertime, the sound of glass being cut would surge out of the windows and drench the courtyard. To mark Julius's position as the local glass-maker, the shutters on the windows of the ground-floor workshop had been stencilled with the shapes of church windows. Most people worked at the university or at one of the important institutes in the hills but there were more than enough churches, as well as libraries, to keep Papa occupied at a pace that suited him. His main occupation, as far as his little girl ever saw it, was balancing his glass of Sunday weinschorle on his head for her amusement. The squeaks from Ute whenever he dotted the end of her nose with his shaving soap.

Papa's workshop was one thing but the family residence upstairs had been a haven of perfect modesty and order dominated by a polished oval dining table. The lamps were angular and in gobstopper colours. All plants were ruthlessly policed. Whenever she couldn't sleep, and wherever she was, on their travels or at home in The Hide's custom-made bed, Ute returned to Bauamtsgaße's cornet-shaped pillows and pine-framed single beds. In her mind, they had grown more comfortable as time had passed.

Appearances were the price you paid for an orderly life. Not until she lived with a man who would spend an entire day whipping cream had Ute thought any of this to be unusual.

And Mama had been telling the truth—there was indeed a lot of recycling. The newspaper lying open on the old dining table was from a week ago. The kitchen was the room Ute remembered, although the glaze on the tiles had dulled, as if the room had been submerged in the amber of a bottle of Rheingau wine. The furniture was as she remembered it, too, in that she feared it had not been aired in all that time.

Other families had bibles and book-club copies of *Effi Briest.* The Pfeiffers' shelves used to bear toolboxes and box files knotted with gardener's twine. The shelf for Papa's collection of ecclesiastical reference books now housed a row of photo albums: a kind of photographic retrospective cut out from old albums, magnified and digitised, then printed on paper that was a soupçon too shiny for Ute's tastes. The albums covered with tanned cordovan that someone had pawed and made greasy.

In the tone of someone admiring a child's drawing, she said, —That's beautiful, Mama. When do they begin?

—Birth. 1934. The early ones are his favourite. Summer holidays.

—More recent?

—We stopped taking so many photographs when you left.

Except for a photo of Ute on the funicular to the Königstuhl—which she couldn't remember, and one of her wearing enormous earmuffs at the ice rink on Kornmarkt, which she hated, and one of her and Mama on her eighteenth birthday, which she quite liked—all the pictures were of her father. Mama had made it into the edges of enough frames for Ute to flick through the pages and create a photomontage of re-appropriated ears, arms and elbows.

There was Papa in his Beetle when it had been new, sometime in the early sixties. His left arm adjusting the wing mirror so he could admire himself; as a honey-skinned boy at the summer house in Wilhelmsfeld; and standing stiffly outside Peterskirche as the glass he'd spent three years restoring was being lowered into place, his face painted with worry that the windows would fit. She forgave herself some annoyance about her place in the family's photographic history—either Papa was only interested in himself, which was the prerogative of a man of eighty or, God forbid, he needed some help in recognising himself—before coming up with an idea for something they could do as a family.

—I could take some new photographs.

—Please wait until you see him.

—So we'll have something more recent.

—Wait until you see him, I said.

—I have a new phone, there's a very good camera on it.

—Do you have a new father?

She felt herself smiling at the thought of the redemptive conversations you were supposed to have with your mother.

—What does Dr Reuter say?

—A stroke, a small stroke, more than one. Maybe a little Parkinson's, some dementia.

A little of everything, then. Like Tort at the breakfast buffet.

—And what else?

—That Julius is in his eighties.

There were the sounds of a struggle. Papa's breathing would have been audible from the street and, when he appeared, she would not have recognised him were it not for the fact that he had just left his own bedroom and become agitated at the sight of a stranger in his living room.

—Papa, she said, to a frown from her mother.

Whatever was going on he didn't like it. He struggled to extend his hand towards Ute's and then let it tremble in the air, staring through it as if it were a reading glass.

When she was a little girl, Papa—taller than Tort by far and wider than a builder's van—had more of the look of a butcher than a maker of stained glass. There were whiskers on cheeks red as a radish; under his beret the creamy, kissable skin on his bald head; pince-nez clinging to caveman's ears. Button-fastened braces supported chair-worn corduroy. Behind his ear, completing the picture, would be a carved Staedtler pencil. As far as appearances and first impressions would allow this had been a well-mannered man in a drama free world.

Mama offered a drink and Ute accepted. Anything else would have been an insult.

—Does he take any exercise? Ute said. He looks to have seized up.

—Your father is doing very well.

—I wish you'd told me.

—We are busy here. You are busy too.

Papa started to speak, but one word couldn't find the next. There was no more recognition between them to speak of and at first Ute saw only faint traces of it between Papa and Mama. Gently her mother led him to one of their kitchen chairs where he sat panting, bare feet scuffing the broken tiles. As Mama moved methodically around him, Papa allowed her to wipe his mouth, bumping his head against her hand. He started to burp and giggle and Ute couldn't help but stare.

Papa sipped his apple juice and she took hers with her, glad of something to hold as she paced the floor, sifting through some bits and pieces on the old oval dining table. There were some leaflets describing the services of the glass-maker and an old card advertising a performance of *St Matthew Passion* at Peterskirche on Easter 1994, not long before she left home. She understood that the card should stay where it was.

Mama intercepted her gaze, but instead of reproaching Ute, she smiled.

—You can see that life has become a little challenging for us.

The smile said they were on a new footing.

Papa was an obstinate old man with a child's chary eyes, and, without any say in the matter, they had all become new people. His pyjama trousers were soaked through and there was egg—possibly—on his shirtfront. The smack of his lips as he savoured the apple juice which Mama said he drank at the same time every day.

The Pfeiffers' daughter perchance. The wary eyes on her had to belong to Julius. The bailiff disapproval was all Christa, and the nice look of the nunnery. The little beak on her twitching.

The Pfeiffers were handy enough as far as landlords went. Christa was a quick little creature well acquainted with austerity, and Julius the glass-maker as charismatic as dungarees allowed. The big bacony head on him, and the walrus-moustache, tint attributable to many good years at the cheroots.

Home was, or used to be, Julius's old workshop.

In one way or another, Seanie was always around the place, half-arsedly taking care of the niceties: the walks with Julius to the old bridge; a nice sit abroad in the yard; a flick of the photo albums; a peel of an orange, a bit of porridge on occasion, if Christa was ever under the weather. Sometimes Julius spoke in dialect, often decipherable and often not. There was the sense that if he wasn't talking to Seanie he wasn't talking to anyone.

Down Seanie went last week with a gift from the shitey Greek holiday. Julius brought the honey jar up to his watery eye, mouth open and staring into the depths. With no reason apparent Christa gave Seanie a kiss.

Were they that gone on honey? Or they were as lonely as Hannah's hen.

Another hour before he was due at the Europäischer Hof for the first passenger of the day. A bit of breakfast would sort him out.

A cup of tea, he'd be unstoppable.

Their place had small little glass elves dancing on the walls, stained glass in the bathroom, in the hall, on the walls, and on the kitchen floor. The kitchen lights, fixed to the wall and going nowhere, had very little of what you might call power to them.

The sounds as you moved around, not the best of acoustics.

Next door, the bed looked warm as buttered toast. The tea on the tray was weak as a puddle, as requested. But Hannah was in no mood to hear the latest about the hen. The poor hen could only lay so many, and apparently someone (the same someone who was supposed to have moved out days ago) was eating too many eggs.

—What's a good amount, egg-wise?

—One egg.

She might have called the police on him for blackguarding eggs.

For it hadn't been the best of summers. The holiday just past, an all-inclusive around the Aegean, was supposed to be their way of letting all that go by. Hannah'd been as stressed as one of the leukaemia mice in her lab. She wanted holiday feet. Each morning she would horse on the baby oil before gowling on about the cost of the add-on spirits. Seanie meanwhile was easily reconciled with the no-name rum.

One sunny morning, after an unsatisfactory boat shower, on the cabin's 140cm double bed she said, —I'm late.

Late seemed to mean a blue line and a holy fuck.

—Seanie, please tell me what we will do with a baby?

Easy the answer, and easy the feeling in him. There'd be the three of them in it now. A little fat Heidelberger, a paddling pool in the Pfeiffers' yard. Shyly Seanie spoke his heart, as if on a ledge and in their dying moments.

To the sky and the Aegean wide he said, —I won't be found wanting.

Hannah was quiet, pale and drawn. Most certainly, the next morning quiet and the next morning quiet.

The morning after came the change in the news. Smoke without fire. On her way to the sun deck, she said, —You wouldn't have known the first thing to do with a child.

The days began scampering across his mind: the blue line and the holy fuck. In the forlornest tone possible, she'd said, —We have to talk.

Out of Seanie came the kind of soft, surprised Oh you make when you slop too much milk into the tea. The ha'penny dropped then. They were going to come to an arrangement. Seanie not being there when they got home was the arrangement. He was being given the road.

—Was it anything I did? he said.

—Or didn't do.

He'd about worn a hole in the deck going up and down to say indecipherable sorries and goodbyes. He asked were there others. There weren't, but there would be.

Now Hannah drained the tea, and more was poured on the double. She wanted to know when exactly he'd be off. She'd have his bags ready and would he mind clearing out the fridge? He could take the mint sauce.

In the dull heat of the morning, the reply died in his mouth.

Dad's Donegal suit for the chauffeuring, dead man's suit cinched at the waist just the job.

Seanie was taking it slow before work, slowly stepping through the air, fathoming the Neckar, its meek sway, and a pair of rowers pulsing through it. The river, was anything down there apart from pike and anacondas, Goebbels and shopping trollies and all the rest? A long walk off a short pier, being hauled out on a riverbank somewhere in bastard Liechtenstein.

Float through the darker channels for more than a minute, and you could count on a call from home. She'd been on already, but you were as well asking for a clatter about the head than answering before nine in the morning.

—You having a summer? Dead here.

—The storms would take the head off you. Then it's like nothing happened.

—Well for you. There's hogweed up through the kitchen floor. I'll wake up strangled by it some morning. If your father was here, he'd know what to do.

—He'd say get someone in, Mam.

—Lot of use you are. And some shower them Germans. Suppose they know they're going to win, they do? They've the look of people who're going to deliver you a beating.

—This win was a long time coming.

—You reckon?

—I do.

—How much?

—Any money.

—Steady on, she said.

Seven–one was seven–one for a finish. People not much given to excitement had been finding the smiling getting the better of them. But optimism was lethal in the wrong hands.

—What do you know about football, pray tell?

—Been picking bits up, pray tell, he said.

—It's your ideas you'd want to be picking up. I'll tell you why they won. You know what they did for themselves. They took their own water. They took German water to South America. I'd be inclined to say that gives them an unfair advantage. And you a Brazilian trying to run your own business, and Bavarians showing up places with their own bottles of water.

—I think they stick to their hotel.

—Bring their own mattresses as well. Their own Hoovers. All of this says to me they're not going home without the cup. That's as clear as night. It's all in the mind, that's where success stories begin. The new doctor told me I feed on negative thinking. What do you think of that? My own doctor calling me a battleaxe? But when a man like that talks you have to listen, on account of them being straight with you. Which is a rarity. So the news is I'm on a different path. I'm expressing gratitude.

—I've a nice positive thought for you. I'm working this morning.

—Butter wouldn't melt.

—A bit of driving, chauffeuring. Dignitaries.

Mam's answer amounted to: who am I, a fucking mental patient?

But Seanie'd found himself a bit of part-time work in getting said dignitaries to and from a conference at the old university. Nobel-prize winners, aged science types with wastrel hair, a procession of them with helplessness the general air. Not a great deal of eye contact in the Laureate world. Gazes trained on the rooftops in case of minute adjustments to the cosmos.

He was a great believer these days in the universe, and a great believer in its cruelty. Mam's keratoconjunctivitis, her Yankee candles, his father's ashes left in a lump by the Standing Stone. Seanie of late was a great believer, too, in miracles, the great miracle of the body. His hair was long lamented, a fine head of it at thirty-one, bald as a hen's egg at thirty-two. Out in clumps it came. Dad'd said it took the wild look off him.

Each week Mam was duty bound to ask, —How's the diploma?

What got to him always was the tone: Come out of the way there, Seanie. The want about you, would you ever get it seen to?

For our hero had spoofed his way through two undergraduate degrees and a master's. Depending on the time of the day, he was or wasn't about to start doing a PhD in metaphysical poetry. He could speak, he could read, five languages. At home, in Cloonfad, they called him Google Translate. Speaking all those languages would make him an excellent diplomat, Mam had said. Or an excellent barman, according to his dad, landlord of the pub Seanie was born above.

—Not a diploma exactly. But it's on hold while I figure a few things out. While me and Hannah figure a few things out.

—Hannah and I. And why should we all suffer while you float through life?

The call ended then, Mam saying something about checking Dad's grave for hogweed.

It was a bank holiday he died. Days after finishing the Airtricity half-marathon in a personal best, Noel Donnellan was stone dead of a heart attack.

They'd been all weekend at the pints, tempers rising. Whenever he lost the head it was like spicy beans being forced into Seanie's larynx. There'd been word that someone had got into a snot and gone into the kitchen at Donnellan's and taken hold of a baking tray (the one they used for turkeys) and he'd flung it through the window of Tony Mannion's taxi.

The talk about the place was he lamped his own father, that Seanie Donnellan had sat down to his pint after hopping Noel in the head with the baking tray.

Mam said she knew by looking at him that Seanie done it, from his mien: freshly cast out of Eden, tender, a maddened dog. She'd felt it in her spine but the bare truth of it was that this messer hadn't touched anyone.

Dad was dead of fright anyhow, giving new meaning to the phrase you'll be the death of me. Before the month's mind was out, Seanie, who could have been a diplomat or a barman, got reefed out of the place.

He took himself off to Germany. Nothing to his name apart from one of Dad's old deodorants and an anthology snatched from the bedside.

Lo, a man of letters was born.

Haunting the antiquarians, flinging out the poetry left, right and centre. Not above stealing books either, the pale purple, the lilac of poetry, the cool blues of the novel, the deep greys of the essay, the wild fucking blackness of his brain without someone else's thoughts to fill it.

You'd see him above on the Holy Mountain, on the Philosophers' Walk half-rising into the sky. The heart sunken into him. Helplessly talking to the dead dad. A hallucination, you might have called it, a gentle hallucination always. Bold as brass Dad would appear, drinking a bottle of tea to himself on Untere Straße.

He'd make appearances in the boudoir, too, so to speak. He had a great snout for altercations in the sack. Fine woman that Hannah, he'd say, if you could only keep up with her. I'd be inclined to ask if she had any sisters.

Other times Noel Donnellan was pure philosophy, pure nature boy.

A geography teacher in his day, before hearing the call of the saloon, and a bar with his name above the door. A certain stool in Donnellan's, him being a certain Donnellan. The first brown dinner of the day eaten in the bar, get the news and in company reflect upon it. Not before muting the Angelus, a small bowl of sponge and custard, and home then for the other dinner, the first dinner being purely ceremonial. Afterwards, elements notwithstanding, out to the garden. For Noel Donnellan's roses people came all the way across north Connacht. His way of calling you friends was giving out cuttings. An acre of garden, a house, the pub with his name above the door, yet in the greenhouse he'd spend all of August. The tomatoes colouring, Noel cooing them into being. It was a fine balance with the calcium shortages and the potassium. Hosepipe ban? Fuck your hosepipe ban. Noel Donnellan had a greenhouse to look after. He would have to be coaxed out of there with the last of the tomatoes for ripening on the sill. The jumper on and back to the bar for the Angelus and the remote control. Summers were for plants and foolishness, autumns for oblivion. You wouldn't see him for the real dinner. Nothing in him apart from a small tin of ravioli every other day. By no means an alcoholic, Noel Donnellan hating drinking seemed to be the point of it all. Off it again after Christmas dinner, relieved to hit the top of the year, and a new man by the Epiphany. Seed catalogues coming in from left and right. From Holland they came. Better Boys, Creoles, Big Boys, Early Girls, Brandy Wines, Celebrities, Lemon Boys. Oxhearts. Above all it was the variety in the tomato world that would keep you going.

Taking Julius to the Vineyard

There were no thunderstorms forecast, and Mama said they'd take a drive to the Philosophers' Walk to check on the fruit. Ute used to love Sundays up there, the thrill of completing some task before proudly interrupting her father to seek further instruction, or to be submitted to a gentle but important-at-the-time lesson about vine management; under threat of reproach if she was unable to replicate her father's particular way of thinning foliage.

But Papa did not look ready to be outdoors at all. He was wearing his house slippers and someone thought it had been a good idea to dress him in trousers above his pyjamas. He hadn't shaved around his whiskers, which he had always done. Rakish and louche and only a little unhinged.

In the struggle to get Papa dressed, Mama mustn't have had time to think about what she was going to wear herself. They were his old trousers, the corduroys pale with wear.

—Are they his?

—I buy them for both of us at the same time.

Ute didn't say, You could at least get a belt that fits. You used to be so smart. Mama used to wear such beautiful things.

There seemed to be no recognition that they had moved location to the garage. Any inkling that Papa might still have been able to drive was banished by his attempt to get into the passenger seat without first opening the door. Getting him up off the ground and into the car took about twenty humbling minutes, during which time Mama frowned from the driver's seat and Ute felt a paroxysmal annoyance in being left to deal with her father alone.

—When did Papa stop driving?

—After he drove through the bus stop on Bismarckplatz. The police paid us a visit.

—You never told me that.

—I would have told you.

If she'd asked. Yes, Ute understood.

Properly cared for, which the Beetle was not, these cars were something to behold. The interior smelled like a cat's litter box, the back window struggling as Ute complainingly undid the clip and pushed it out. In the ashtray she saw some scraps of paper, white like mouse droppings. She willed herself not to make a snap judgement. Ute had smoked dope herself from time to time—as a teenager on the riverside during the fireworks at the schloß—and now there was the tempting thought of numbing herself to the rest of the morning.

—Mama, I think someone has been smoking marijuana in the car.

—I know.

Ute continued in the most right-minded tone to which she had access. —You should ask whoever it is to clear up after themselves.

—Why would I do that?

Perhaps it was her repeated looks in the rear-view mirror, but all of a sudden Mama had a licentious air to her. The thought of her mother losing control of the car concerned Ute enough to ask if someone had already been smoking this morning.

—The answer is no.

—I had to ask. We are about to drive somewhere.

—Once a week. And that's it for your questions.

There were more, the most pressing of which: from whom did the drugs come? Did those people come to the house, and what else did they do there, what else did they bring? But the process of her mother smoking drugs in the garage seemed to involve the peculiar man in the wool suit.

—I met him. He was in a big car.

—He should learn to drive it, Mama said. His girlfriend rents the workshop from us.

—He nearly drove over a hen.

—Oh my.

—Do you know the hen?

—It's hers. She treats it like a baby.

Ute was about to leave it there. Another Irish man!

Talking with Irish people was too easy, as if conversation was supposed to be undemanding and its contents inconsequential. Tort had always been charming, a telling word that was absent from her vocabulary until Ute moved to Dublin, when she discovered that the Irish do a good job of snuggling up to you and appearing confidential while seeking ways to take advantage of you.

In addition to being helpful, if a little hopeless, around the place, her mother told her that Seanie spent occasional weekday afternoons with Papa up at the vineyard. Seanie never did much work, as Ute would see when she got there, but he was dependable and undemanding company for her father, and this was precisely what Papa needed.

Ute liked the sound of Seanie and her father together, but Mama said there was something wrong with him that he should have so many afternoons at his disposal.

—What does he do, Mama?

—Nothing.

—He has to do something. That is a very big car.

—That's not his.

—He must have it for a reason.

—Not necessarily. I hear him talking to your father about books, and going to university, but I've never seen him go anywhere. He says he's taking the scenic route. His answer changes every time you ask.

—At least he's not doing something.

—Which is the same as doing nothing. His girlfriend is our tenant, I could tell you what she does.

—I don't need to know about her.

—She's a lab technician. We don't accept people without a permanent position.

—He's very bald. For one so young.

—His date of birth will be in the rental agreement. If you really want to know.

—Not really.

This was a lot of questions for not really.

And Ute might have laughed too. For any sane person would have wanted to find a man with an allotment and a government job. That she might one day marry someone else born in the Sankt Elisabeth hospital was as likely as Ute dating the Imam of Schwetzingen mosque. Until now, she had demonstrated to the world that when it came to choosing lovers—and sticking with them, and failing to leave them when that was all she wanted to do—she had needed her head examined.

This Seanie, she could easily imagine being as irritated by him as she had been by Tort, and this of course had nothing to do with what he did for a living or his age. He was the wrong age for her, and would at best be a means to an end. And this was the most appealing phrase she had heard in a very long time.

After lunch, Ute sat outside and took care of the job she had been putting off for months. She composed an email to explain why she would not be submitting any more work for the newspaper. Above her desk, Ute's editor, Margaret, had a poster that urged them all forward with the slogan 'Failure is not an option'. As far as Ute was concerned, failure was always an option.

As a sign of the times, she had been encouraged to come up with articles about meals to be made with a kettle and a sack of lentils. Writing about anything, let alone thrift, was not Ute's idea of a fulfilling day at work, but she was aware that not everyone who works talks about fulfilment. They have other things on their minds. In the note, she said that she was making a polite exit from writing, and that, as she'd always done, she'd find other things to do—other ways of expressing herself. She had long since decided that who she was had very little do with self-expression.

She sent the email—that would show them—safe in the knowledge that she would be spared a reply. Now, Tort was calling from the home number. There was no possibility that he could see her, or the state of the yard, but that was the first thing that crossed her mind.

—You first, she said. You went out without saying anything.

—It's not going to hurt you to tell me where you are, he said. I heard long beeps.

—I've gone home.

—I don't see you anywhere. Unless you're playing hide-and-seek.

It was a relief when the line grew buzzier and Tort started to sound far away and just a little lonely. She wasn't going to say any more for one reason. Tort's way of listening—with the greedy breaths of a deep-sea diver—usually consumed everything around him. He would deafen her, and madden her, but most of the time she could put up with being deafened and maddened because when they first met Ute had wanted to belong to him, or someone. She was not meant to belong to herself.

And she had a type: deafening, maddening.

—I'll join you, he said. We'll turn it into something. Vienna. Prague is a drive away. Berlin, if you must. Or, I've a mind for a Nuremberg sausage.

Tort was always too fat and the colour of his face had lately risen, from all the food and alcohol, to a varnished teak.

—Why don't you go on a trip? she said. I need to be in one place.

—You're the only person I know who gets a kick out of not moving.

It was Tort who would plan and pay for these glossy trips—Salzburg and Sydney in the last month alone. He'd present them as her idea but it was he and not Ute who was so keen on flying halfway around the world for a concert. A normal person would say that she did not particularly enjoy music. Instead, at home, Ute crept around silencing radios.

Just as it must have weakened him, Tort seemed to have grown to depend on the diet of systematic care she had imposed on him: the breakfast cake baked last thing at night, the new pair of pyjamas to go with the hundreds of others, August gazpacho come rain or shine, sex virtually on demand. In other words, how could she describe his love for her in any other way than weakness?

There seemed to be interesting things happening in the general area of the speedometer. Mama couldn't have known that she was being observed, or else she wouldn't have winced at every passing car and yelped every time she saw a stop light. Her sigh indicated they were nearing the turn for the Philosophers' Walk.

Ute's phone buzzed again. The garden at The Hide was Tort's way of getting through to her. The courgettes had come into flower this week—and she'd been unapologetic at how much she loved the dapper stripes on the courgette, the suggestiveness of the stamens, and the blossoms themselves, which were too golden and ceremonial-seeming for her to think of as food. In the pictures that he was sending her, a few of the courgettes were running to marrow, and the flowers, which normally she'd have snipped off with surgical care, had begun to mope.

Why don't you pick them? she texted.

The reply came: we're waiting for you to come home.

We're? was her reply.

She called but Tort's line was busy. She called again. She called a number of times but didn't leave a message.

Throughout all of this, her father was staring at his knees, jiggling something in his pocket. He glanced at her once, nothing more. And Tort, who liked to talk and talk and talk, was using another kind of silence against her. What good would it do him? In games as a child, Ute could always hide longer than any of the other children. She could wait anyone out.

She was twenty-four when they met and he was forty. She was a waitress in Andrew Edmunds in Soho and thus she had a role to play. Then, as in the future, she deferred to Tort's highly coloured reaction to the wine she had poured.

—Riesling means pebbles, he'd said. Wet rocks.

Ute, being the daughter of a winemaker, wanted to blurt that wine was fermented grape juice and nothing more—how could it be?—but, angling for a tip, she murmured something bland and appropriate to Tort's puckered lips. He went on to praise her judgement so effusively that Ute's boss, Neal, the man who had chosen the Riesling in the first place, became jealous. This tickled her more than she ever thought it would.

Ute didn't suppose she'd ever see him again but back Tort came the following night and the one after, her night off. She had hesitated when Neal called her at home with news that the big, fat, rich Irish bastard was back, and would she come in just to humour him? Since it was her night off, Neal would bend the rule that said employees were not supposed to join guests at their tables. Tort, of course, couldn't grasp that Ute wasn't working and kept on asking her to fetch him things to eat. The wine was so very wet on its own. And she felt, as she'd felt so many times before, a great unease and consequential excitement, and had to ask him what he meant when he asked her all about herself.

He asked her out so clumsily—a rose was involved—that it broke her heart.

They never had a name for their relationship. They never dated, they were never boyfriend and girlfriend, calling themselves partners didn't stick. Ute just called him 'my man', which turned out to be the thing that melted his heart and broke hers, especially when it was said during the uninteresting but effective sex that he always made too much of. There was no name for that either. At least there was no calling it lovemaking, and, in this, they were alike. Tort didn't much like to kiss—and nor did she—but they kissed six, five, four times a day and so on until they arrived at the mutually agreeable routine of once a week, always in the mid afternoon, always with him behind her, and always somewhere comfortable. People hardly seemed to have sex in beds anymore but dining tables and aeroplane toilets were not for people of their dimensions.

Later she would say that she had fallen in love with his Beethoven head and the size of him—Tort was an oak barrel with flamingo legs—for she had never slept with a man she hadn't made herself fall in love with, not in any calculated sense. She was surprised at the change that occurred in the process, by her decision to turn captive; right down to wearing heels when she was not a heel person, when she knew the damage they did to your feet.

They occupied London as only tourists and wealthy people, and those associated with them, can do; even though it took her a few visits to realise that you didn't bring your own towels and soap to a five-star hotel. She had not been made for places like London. One day Tort came home from a meeting with some Irish government people at The Connaught. Ireland had had one monstrous recession and the economy had recovered enough, and the people were showy enough, for it to be on its way to another. By the weekend, they were in a rented house with a stained-glass cupola and no kettle.

In their first few weeks in Ireland, they didn't eat in a restaurant without Tort trying to buy it. He never spoke about what was on his mind, except about what he was about to buy, take, or get. Some things—comfort, and stuff, there was always stuff—were more important than love.

She was not made for Dublin either. The act of splurging on dinners became a theatrical scenario. Desmond 'Tortoise' Kinsella booked tables and signed cheques under a nickname, which he had given himself for the frames on his glasses and the supposedly leisurely way he went about activities from negotiating contracts to dealing with the never-ending courses in the restaurants expensive enough to justify his custom. There he would eat as fast as he did at home, or faster perhaps, always eager for the bill, which he would never sign without cracking his knuckles. She tried not to blame him for the fact that he should have been forced to wear a bib as well as a napkin to eat. There had already been occasions when she had considered taking a plate to the bathroom and eating there, away from his lip-smacking and his way of pursuing the food around the plate. She noticed this from the start yet said nothing, which is why Ute told herself that she might love him. But Tort made it clear that wasn't necessary, as long as they could play along until such time as she might.

Everything else was negotiable, including his proposals, which came around more often than tax bills. Often she caught him staring at her ring finger, as if something were missing. But marriage in her world implied children, and not parenting was the least the granddaughter of a well-known eye surgeon could do for the world.

Up on the Philosophers' Walk, there were the familiar astrophysicists on their fold-up bicycles and orange-skinned pensioners who could have passed for ageing tennis professionals. This part of Neuenheim had always been moth-eaten, grandparenty, embassy-like, at best—if astrophysicists could ever be mistaken for diplomats. But a sheen of wealth was apparent as it hadn't been before. Everything west of there looked as though it had been rewired, re-plumbed, sand-washed, stuccoed, and looked showy and unapproachable and also not.

Their main residence was an hour away in wine country, but the Völker-Steins kept a house at Philosophenweg, No 1. Felix Stein was a former schoolteacher who had used his wife's money to invest in an enterprise software company that had gone global while remaining quietly sequestered near their hometown. The family were now so rich, according to Papa, that Felix could give away billions without it seeming to matter to his lifestyle, which, the way people described it, was that of a sultan. The Sankt Hedwig was just one of his many playthings: football teams or the scientific research that tickled his fancy at the time. Philanthropy was a powerful but abstract concept for a teenage girl but Ute's true fascination had always been with Felix's wife, Dorothee.

The last time Ute saw them, at Papa's retirement party, Dorothee Völker-Stein made sure to be the life and soul of the party. She had copper-toned hair cut into an asymmetric fringe that, when no one in Heidelberg cut their hair in that way, gave her the demeanour of a fetishist. With a laugh that never quite began and never quite ended, she had been fascinated by Ute. Her work, her plans, her friends, her boyfriend. Dorothee was the only person who had ever called Tort Ute's boyfriend.

The Völker-Stein residence—Ute had been in it only once, a seven-year-old in need of the bathroom—was up high behind the battlements whose coral-red sandstone, she liked to think, would have been there since the time of the monks on the Holy Mountain.

—They've cleaned up at last, Mama said.

Mama said Felix Stein had spent a year and a million euros on a new parking garage for the maid's car. Every stone in the wall had been numbered, removed and replaced around an entirely new set of foundations.

—I'm not sure this hill can survive everything they're doing to it.

—It's quite a substantial hill, Ute said. And it's been there a while. Perhaps they know what they're doing.

—That's what you say until the entire thing collapses under them.

The row of garages, built into battlements as long as a street in Mayfair, was open to reveal a column of Bentleys, Maseratis and vintage Jaguars, as well as a single Mini, the maid's presumably—the cars had one of the best views in Heidelberg. The noon sun, insistent as a siren, gleamed on the river. A full coal barge, its flags limp, barely stirred the water. Somewhere in that picture was Bauamtsgaße, and the Pfeiffers. Mama with her marijuana, and Papa with his photo albums and a view of very little apart from the courtyard, proudly unbeautiful and garnished with weeds and sweepings that his wife had been ignoring as if to prove a point. All because Ute had not been home in so long.

Mama rammed a line of bikes and parked the Beetle, deliberately it had to be assumed, more or less in a hedge. She hauled Papa out of the car and down the stone steps and winding path to the vineyard's great brown door. On the steps Ute saw enough fallen plums—split and offalesque in their suggestiveness—to make a substantial batch of jam, the odour pointing to the fact that they were already midway to fermentation and being redefined as wine.

Papa always used to say he was quite rich for such a poor man. But the Pfeiffers were neither poor nor rich, they were normal. Due to the age of the vines, the yields were low, even in a good year. In those good years, the harvest would produce one thousand bottles of a wine called Promise Me the Mountain—but Ute couldn't remember a good year, and she had never reasoned why Papa, never one for fancy, had given the wine such a whimsical name.

Papa's wine was a basic wine, he was always happy to admit. Basic is my personal guarantee, he would say. As basic as the entrance to our home, which must be clean and well lit and safe under foot. Basic.

Help was always available to plough the steep hillside—he used a winch to ferry the grapes up to his cabin—but he never wanted any. Sometimes he pretended he enjoyed

Mama's company in the vineyard but it was never his ideal situation. His ideal situation involved having a proper vineyard like the Völker-Steins', and therefore didn't exist. Felix Stein owned the mansion on the Philosophers' Walk, a manor house and a vineyard in Forst as well as the Sankt Hedwig boat, which was so small and exclusive as to amount to a conspiracy of some sort—a private joke between Felix Stein and the rest of the world. Exclusivity came at a price, too. They were supposed to be great friends with the Völker-Steins, but Papa and Mama rarely went to the boat.

At the vineyard, Papa seemed to be willing himself towards words. It was July, and the flowers would have bloomed. The grapes were green and hard to the touch but beginning to ripen. They had been waiting silently for Papa to come and here he was. He took a hoe and cut a slice of earth and grass smaller than one of his photo albums. Combing through it deftly, his big fingers danced. For the first time today, he seemed to be observing a living object rather than mid-air.

Papa sniffed the sod, nibbled a little then spat it out, his soil-black tongue darting in and out. Not half an hour ago, he'd been lying on the floor of the garage.

Ute retreated to the gate. The vineyard had gotten so wild as to make their presence negligible. No ploughing, no grass management nor pruning nor any tying-back whatsoever.

—Do you have help? she said.

—Markus looks after the place. Perhaps he could do a little more. If I see him I will say something. He's never here in the day.

—Markus is still in Heidelberg?

—He's still here.

—Is he still painting?

—After a fashion, Mama said.

Ute went to take the sod from Papa.

—Leave him, Mama said.

Only after some pressing did she mention that Markus had suffered a nervous breakdown in his first year at art school and painting now formed part of his therapy at the Sankt Thomas Home where he spent his time as an in-patient. An insomniac, as well as everything else, he often spent entire nights at the vineyard.

As a teenager Markus was always going to be a full-time painter and spoke the names of English art schools—St Martin's, the Slade—like they were local bus stops. He ignored Papa's offer of an apprenticeship at the glass-maker's. Instead, he spent all his free time sketching Ute. At first, it was copies of *The Hare* by Dürer, which with practice became her face transposed onto a hare's face, which became Ute with hare's eyes, which, once his nerve had grown, became Ute with her own face and her own eyes. Ute as seen by Markus was less expressive than she saw herself but her features also had more clarity—all Markus's work on eyes had paid off. He told her that he had counted her freckles, and that all over her body she had one hundred and five.

Papa blundered towards the former centre of his little winemaking operation, barging about while waving his arms as if shooing pigeons. Then he did something Ute had never seen anyone do before. Still waving his arms, he began to chant under his breath while performing a gentle sort of war dance.

—Should he go and sit in the car?

—He wants to be here. He wants to see you. Have a look around.

The cabin made such an eerie picture—the fermentation tank turned on its side and lying empty, as if awaiting commemoration—that Ute considered how long they would be able to hold onto this place. The once sturdy structure now looked like it might disintegrate and, now that the basket press had been dismantled, the interior resembled the scene of an interrupted burglary.

She felt her father would not be happy if he knew they were all there, which, she supposed, he didn't. But now, like some kind of maestro, he was with upturned palms conducting another conversation.

—He's directing a choir, Mama said. At Peterskirche.

Ute wished her mother had saved him the bother and anguish of this day out, although she did wonder what he saw when he looked at the buckets filled with last year's wet leaves. Perhaps he was seeing lily ponds, she didn't know. Papa moved to the door of the cabin. Was he inspecting the shelves, inwardly listing their contents as if in preparation for an inventory? Ute thought of all the possessions her father had accumulated but could not now remember—diamond grinders, drills and band saws, soldering irons. He had spent many decades arranging his workshop and this cabin as neatly as filing cabinets and now, if you had asked him where it was, he wouldn't have been able to answer. Nor would he have been able to find a thing, not a single watering can.

Mama stepped back so that Ute could join Papa at the door. She mimed her fascination at the scene before accepting the tools—secateurs and a broken hoe—that he began piling into her arms.

—What shall I do with these?

—Play along, Mama said. And then we can go.

Rather than the anticipated scorn, Mama's face was flushed with tenderness. —You weren't to know.

All of a sudden Papa was talking slowly, and in a low voice.

It was 1943 and he was a boy. He was young and glad to be alive, even though he was scared of most things, what people thought above all. He was worried about Germany, his country, for he cared for its good name. He was brave for saying so. He was pulling his life—all those beautiful familiar things—toward him. Now the story moved forwards in time. Papa's voice was clear but he was speaking in a good approximation of an Irish accent and he was talking to Ute softly and easily about Ireland.

The story took a little following at first: Papa was flying around north County Galway as if he had seen it for himself. Birds were skittering in the wind. He had just walked home in slanting rain. There would be a decent growing season this year but he was anticipating a brutal winter. Winter and not summer was the time for sport. Sport was a useful distraction—in fact, it was more than a distraction, it was the only news worth reporting and it was such a pity that they hadn't made it into the World Cup.

—Does he know what's going on with the football? Ute said.

—Of course.

Now she had it! Papa did know someone from Ireland. And something then occurred to her that she had not expected and could not deal with. Her father recognised her, no, he had warmed to her because in this state he thought Ute might be someone else. Papa thought she was his new friend, the young man who lived downstairs in the old workshop.

The Laureate

Today's Laureate came splay-footed across the lobby of the Europäischer Hof. The head boiled off him, a face like a gas explosion, and not much in the way of a good morning.

Trust Seanie to meet the one man in the whole of Germany with no notion of football. Italian, making it worse. And he'd no interest in the toffees Seanie kept for the VIPs.

On the way to the car, Prof. Dr Tomasso Benedetto made it quite clear that they'd be going nowhere near Universitätsplatz. The Laureates were expected to be in or around the Neue Universität building all day (for lunch there was to be an important carp buffet), but the Laureate had more than done his bit: a working breakfast with Sir Q. Richard E. Grieve, he'd listened at some length to Lesley Beverly Wainwright's particular views on blue light. Enough was enough.

Ploughed his own furrow then, this handsome pope of a man in Wayfarers and safari suit. Looking seventy but virile as, the saucy musk off him. Seanie knew his type, his type was the type to attempt intercourse with a tree from a high-speed train. But it wasn't every day the man who co-discovered knockout mice wanted you to take him on a drive around the town.

—What do you know about Albert Speer? he said.

—Try me.

—Where is his house?

—In all my life, I've never been up there.

—In all your life? the Laureate said. What is this, all my life?

Seanie was the soft mark always. But his nickname at home was Google Translate not Google Maps.

—I can take you to the place where Mark Twain stayed. Or the school where Oscar Wilde's children studied.

He knew well the location of the school. Often, on his quieter days, he'd eavesdrop on the guided tours that trundled through the altstadt. But he was not well acquainted with the house of Albert Speer, who may have been as much part of the place as the phone shops or the burnt-out synagogue. The bad history, any of that, you just didn't ask.

Seanie looked it up. Speer's house was a short spin away up on Schloß Wolfsbrunnenweg.

—That's where you want to go? Not Universitätsplatz?

—That's what I said.

The splinter of ice in the Laureate's eye.

Up past the castle they drove, the morning settling upon them bleak and malodorous. At Speer's gates, the hanging mist was penitential. A sign: Vorsicht vor dem Hund and hark, a barking dog, a recording played through speakers hung on a pylon. A notorious house, this, and there often had to be visitors at the gates. On its loop went the electronic hund.

—How long are you here? the Laureate said.

—Heidelberg? A year, two.

—You like it?

—Why wouldn't I?

—Germans?

—Better again.

—You like them?

—I do, but putting a bit of rusk in their sausages wouldn't kill them.

—What about Italy?

—What about it?

—The food, it's the best.

—No doubt about it. But you're talking to someone who wouldn't eat lasagne until he was twenty-five. I can speak the language though.

—What do you do when you're not driving? the Laureate said. Science, I take it?

—Poems, Seanie said. I have some Goethe there in the glove compartment.

Seanie'd had his fair share of poetry. His nose forever in the dusty volumes, life a dark, dull business without them, your Donnes, your Marvells strong as poitín. Eyes dancing on the winged chariots and vast eternities. Heart fat and soul organised.

—Are you published?

—Just in my notebook. I'm in the market for a new project.

—I adopted one of Speer's projects as my own when my wife died.

Here we fucking go, a sympathiser. Seanie should have known from the safari jacket.

—I'd like to take a walk. Would you come with me?

The car was abandoned for the fire path, idly the men wandering the forest wilderness, farinaceousness alive in the air. The breaths they took were rich and mealy, and the mealiness was of home. The Laureate, too, was getting wistful in himself.

—When Susie died, every night before bed I made the journey from our house to her childhood home in Texas. Every day in the Spandau prison yard Speer would measure out the distance from Berlin to Heidelberg as he walked, picturing the places he was walking through. It helped me sleep when I did it, so it became a valuable excursion. I live in the United States, so my walk took me from Salt Lake City to Seguin, Texas. Thirteen hundred miles in two months.

Seanie's thoughts fell to an old man walking the prison yard with strain in his heart. The Laureate didn't walk for recreation, nor distraction. Walking for love was a very different order. A sad affair to think of it, a lonely widower pacing his bedroom, the lonely boy stepping in silence over his father's corpse. And it all got the better of our hero then. A certain foolishness became epidemic, coming quickly upon him, stirring in the wires and flowing upwards, the crying and all that. Tears seeping then geysering from the heat of the earth's mantle and from under the forest floor. Throbbing from the deepest geothermal part of him, the store never visited.

Was this a pastime now, the crying?

The Laureate had no notion to go anywhere near Universitätsplatz. Seanie only lost the injured look when it was decided they needed a treat. On the terrace of the Europäischer Hof, there was soup and the like, sandwiches as big as small blocks of apartments. Seanie had a bit of bother with the cocktail stick in his.

—Don't you have to give a talk? he said.

—They've already heard all I have to say. But, since you ask, I will draw your attention to my reason for being in Heidelberg this week. My Nobel Prize, I follow it around the world. My Nobel Prize, which gave me no more pleasure than roasting a lamb for my wife. It gave me no more pleasure than our Sunday mornings, about which I won't elaborate. So when you get to my age you take any human warmth you can get. I'm not going to elaborate. I applaud your, no I applaud you, Seanie. I applaud you. I wouldn't do what you do, go through life without any purpose, but I do admire it. Because you're doing it for love, I think? I hope. It goes without saying that I like you.

People came and went from their table to genuflect. Seanie could just see the Prof. Dr at some other Nobel junket, some science floozy in his lap, her nose damp from his ear. The dead wife chat and the walking to Bumfuck, Texas.

—What now, Seanie? What now? I have done all that I could with my life. When I happened to be born, my mother was in Verona, fighting the fascists. She was not painting, which was what she said she was doing. My grandmother was a painter. Not my mother. There were no canvases. We lived in a chalet near the Alps, and there was no painting. There was no time for her to paint. No time for her to do anything apart from oppose the fascists. They came for her of course. I don't remember when but I remember that she was gone and I went to live in a farm with some friends of hers. On this farm we made everything. We needed nothing. There was a war on somewhere, but not there. I was five years old and I was a baker. That began my interest in yeast and such things. Then something happened, I don't know what. The family asked me to leave. There was no more money.

Seanie'd heard something of this story from Hannah. In certain circles, it was a well-known story. The boy's mother disappeared to protest against Mussolini. She sold her belongings and gave the proceeds to a peasant family to house the infant child while she concentrated on her pamphleteering. The family stole the money and the little boy ended up on the streets of Bolzano, surviving on used coffee grounds from the town's cafés.

Sweat crept like a bloodstain through the Laureate's jacket. It was becoming clear that Seanie was welcome to all the sandwiches.

—I ended up in an orphanage. Every few days I got a wet heel of bread. I remember wanting, never being satisfied. I was used to real bread. Then I lived in a hospital for advanced malnutrition. It was a concentration camp. Lying naked on a mattress on the floor. A little worm. If I had had any clothes I would have run away. One day I did anyway. What do you imagine is worse? Living rough in a city or wild in the country, in the wilderness? This was during the war, so I thought I should avoid the built-up areas. I didn't know why, this was just my instinct. It was probably correct. There was no food anywhere, there was little agriculture. The land was hard with the cold. My skin was burnt red with cold, too, and my fingertips were blue. Then they were black. I am surprised I still have them. There was ice on the inside of my coat, on the inside of my nostrils. Looking back, I do not know the difference between myself and the monsters you see in those movies. So I made my way back to the city, but I got lost and ended up in the wrong place, Bassano Del Grappa. Anyway, it was a city, there were people, and do you know what happened, I met a soldier, an Italian soldier, and do you know what he gave me? Yes, he gave me some grappa. In Grappa. I felt myself warming. I would ask for some now but I can't drink it without crying. He had some bread and we had some of that but I could hardly swallow. I had to ask him to soak it in water like they had done in the orphanage. He was able to accompany me into the barracks so I could get warm by the stove. I lay on the bed. I tried to climb inside the mattress, and it was more comfortable than the mattress in any hotel, let me tell you. There was a nurse, and she gave me some new clothes and a bath and she tried to comb my hair. Can you believe it? In a war, she tried to comb my hair. One day somebody came for me. This woman. My mother. I thought, I didn't think I had a mother. Do you know how crazy that sounds? Not crazy. Not crazy. She was crazy, she was crazy for me. She had been looking a year for me. One day I was a naked boy and then they bought me a small cap with a feather in it. I still have it.

Seanie's lips were moving of their own accord. Well, it was a good story, as soothing as a nice toffee. But the Laureate wanted to go up to his room. His pen was leaking in his pocket and he had tired himself out.

Not a soul to turn to then and the sudden bliss of being alone.

The Reformation

Papa always said that holidays were for people who didn't like where they lived. Once, they went to a farm in the Valepp where Ute saw the deer she had been promised. Another time, even though the Pfeiffers weren't skiers, her parents went skiing in the Alps with the Völker-Steins. Never again. And one February, when she was nearly eight, she and her mama went to Baden-Baden for a weekend and returned home to find her Papa kneeling in the messy yard, normally swept clean as a laundry.

Ute had had a better idea than Baden-Baden anyway. Her parents' friends lived only an hour's drive away and she had wanted to chase their goats and fill her cheeks with their grapes. But Mama had insisted on this trip to the thermal baths, where Ute saw an old man's testicles almost reach his knees.

Heidelberg had not been an exciting town in which to be a little girl, but no one—least of all Lothar Pfeiffer, Ute's grandfather, the surgeon; that was his job—would ever have said that the town hadn't seen its share of bad dreams. But that was how the country worked. Things happened and you moved on. If you crashed your bike on the bridge that ran from Bismarckplatz to the bowery suburb of Neuenheim, as Mama once did, you could have depended on aid from one of the smart young doctors scooting between the institutes.

The other cyclists would have ridden briskly on, safe in the knowledge that in a town like Heidelberg there was no such thing as an emergency, just occasional reminders to be careful. It was the kind of quietly prosperous place in which nonagenarians inveigled old Porsches through the cobbled laneways—all business was conducted at a tenured pace—and a family like the Pfeiffers could, as Papa liked to say, live the unmysterious, good life.

Julius the glass-maker with the little vineyard on the Philosophers' Walk, nurse Christa and little Ute with the squaw's plait, and the family's adored and, as of that afternoon, dead spaniel Berti.

The cobbles in the yard were furred with moss. Papa had removed a square metre's-worth and piled the stones in the same way he liked to arrange crispbreads. He was a quick shoveller, of soil as well as food, and Ute was slow to realise that even though her father was digging with his bare hands he wasn't doing any gardening. She had assumed the Tupperware container at his feet was a packed lunch.

—We had no breakfast. Mama was still sleeping.

—Breakfast is the most important meal of the day. No, that's lunch. Or dinner. All meals are important in their own way.

For someone who didn't know how to small talk, Papa was being unusually chatty. Only when Ute called the dog's name, and ran inside to the kitchen to find Berti's basket empty, did she connect Papa's shovelling to something calamitous.

—Where is he?

—Berthold? Papa said. He had to go away.

—Where?

—Away, Mama said.

—Away from here?

—Of course.

—Where?

The way Papa put it, Berti had gone to a house in the country where he could chase all the rabbits he wanted, and without having to worry about traffic. Heaven was never again described so heartily

—Somewhere far away like Baden-Baden, Mama said.

—Baden-Baden isn't so far away. We were there an hour ago.

Papa replaced the last of the cobbles and patted them as though to thank them for their co-operation. Obedient little Berti stones.

There was a picnic table against the wall of an old stable, and Ute took a seat at the bench facing the mossy wall. It was the most beautiful yard in the city and now her dog was buried under it.

When Mama came to sit by her, Ute's end of the bench flew up like a seesaw.

—It's good to go away sometimes, her mother said.

Mama checked the pockets of her cardigan for some toffee or gingerbread to magic the sadness away. She too was making out that the death of a companion—Berti had been so dedicated to his role as Ute's best friend—was a jolly sort of business.

—No toffee today, she said.

There was no way Ute would cry and concede victory so soon.

Mama wasn't a good driver, but she had driven them to and from Baden-Baden and Ute could have done with something to settle her stomach. There would have been a coconut macaroon in the kitchen, unless Papa had eaten them. That was it as far as her mother's attempt to show solidarity—perhaps she thought it wasn't her place, or it should have been Papa's responsibility; since all the mess in the yard was his doing and he was otherwise behaving like they were at a picnic, but without any food.

Her mother began undoing Ute's plait—a low trick, since her mother's hands in her hair was her favourite feeling in the world. This alone soothed her enough to cry, just a little.

She kept her eyes on the wall, both of them overplaying their roles in the pageant in which she, as a defiant survivor of this tragedy, could never forgive Papa, nor Mama for taking her to Baden-Baden in the first place. Theirs was the loveliest courtyard in a town full of lovely courtyards and they should never have left it.

What saved her, a little time later, was a boy older than her but smaller than her. Markus Kaltwasser was blond and pale everywhere, including his beautiful eyelashes. They called him an albino but he wasn't an albino. He was just very pale.

The first thing Ute did was to take his place on the school football team. Until that day, the goal line had been his refuge from the field of play and the other children. Ute—tall and big, even then—cycled a boy's bike and repeatedly asked for a boy's haircut, which she never got. Herr Busch took one look at her and put her in as goalkeeper.

Ute felt guilty for taking his place—their team was strong enough to do without much of a goalkeeper anyway—but Markus didn't seem to mind and kept on appearing at the games to cheer them on, and, when Busch tired of the novelty of a girl in the ranks, Markus declined the opportunity to resume his position in goal.

Ute had never mentioned Berti to anyone else, but Markus seemed to know that she was sickening for something; hence was always available, not to mention—as if he were not used to being in company—always surprised to see her.

It was around that time that Markus brought her a replacement for Berti: a spaniel puppy resembling a woolly cushion he had taken from a family in Neckarhausen. It took some explaining from Papa—animals do not exist to be taken or given away—before the dog was returned whence it came. It wouldn't have been labouring the point to say that there was also something of a tame animal about Markus. He was jittery like a fawn, especially when he thought no one was looking. Most of all she enjoyed him watching her, as though self-consciousness was a not unpleasant side effect of being in love.

Ute thought of herself ready for the world of women and men together. She had after all been to Baden-Baden and witnessed the almost supernatural sight of old men in the nude.

Perhaps she thought of Markus as her boyfriend when she asked, —Have you ever seen anyone naked?

—Myself.

—Anyone else?

The answer came slowly. He had had to think about it.

—My papa.

—I've seen my papa and my mama.

As teenagers, they attended different schools. Markus went to the college on the river—a sure a sign as any that his parents were rich and he was, if not stupid then considered something of a delinquent. Nevertheless, he made it to the gates of her school to walk her home every day. Whenever she saw him there, holding the fruit he'd saved from his lunch, Ute recognised the feeling she had only heard in Mama's favourite song, 'You've Got a Friend'. It had never occurred to her that she had needed one.

Markus was much skinnier than her, but wily thing that she was Ute would feign fatigue so that he would carry her on his back all the way home to Bauamtsgaße. Sometimes she would ask to detour via the old bridge, just in case their first kiss might occur in a place of historical significance.

In preparation, she had been practising her technique on plums and big, fat apples.

On the days when she was carried home Ute would go to bed straight after dinner and the conundrum—the combination of plain foolishness and the epic, altering memory of a piggyback—would keep her awake until dawn. All Markus's sweetness and wariness did was make her anxious for more of it. It made her wary herself, and she started to keep things inside—that she was the only one who understood what it was to be him, the only one.

She'd fallen in love with the world and she was afraid to say that she was not only in love with the world but in love with Markus in it.

His new school backed onto the Philosophers' Walk and the mysterious Holy Mountain. When he said that he drew foxes and wild rabbits from the classroom window, Ute deduced that he spent all his break times alone. The first time he wasn't there to pick her up from school, she found him standing alone by the monkey statue near the bridge. She mimed shaking him by the throat. But Markus was so starved of affection that he seemed to enjoy the pressure on his windpipe.

—Did you forget about me?

—Forget?

—To pick me up.

—Yes.

—What were you so busy doing without me?

Markus shook his head. She did ask him this question a lot. —Have you spoken to anyone all day? she said.

—No one asked me anything.

His feet were turned in, his face was facing away, but she kissed him. The two of them on the bridge just like she had imagined. She could have known this would happen, that he wouldn't like the taste of her, and that by kissing Markus she would turn him into one of the desperate figures in Papa's stained glass. Not a face to fall in love with, exactly—but in his anguish he excited her and again she tried and again he turned his mouth away, this time like she had tried to feed him cold soup. Then he screamed and, after a moment, it became a silent scream, as though the noise now lived in his throat.

Once they'd kissed, what else was there for them to do? For want of any better ideas, they walked home by the river. The Neckar was big and wide and it seemed like a good moment to take his hand. This time he didn't resist.

—Will you be there tomorrow? she said.

—I'm not sure.

—Darling?

Markus didn't hear her say it, or pretended not to—making her wonder if she had said the word at all. She felt brattish, and that the uncertainty was her fault. The evening sun was bouncing off the water and projecting itself onto his pale skin and eyelashes.

—What are the chances?

—Of what?
—Of you being there tomorrow.
—Fifty–fifty.
—Fifty–fifty.

She wasn't five minutes out of the house before she saw him. He was coming up from the river, on his way up to the Heiliggeistkirche and Marktplatz. He didn't look to be in a hurry or was it that his army boots were heavy as anvils? She hadn't seen many clean dreadlocks, but his ropes had wrapped themselves into a filthy pelt as thick as a tree trunk. He had a colt's neck and bright, boy's eyes, but he was a bag of bones, too. The dreadlock was really almost as big as he was.

Ute assumed he was on his way to the Sankt Thomas but, halfway across Marktplatz, Markus turned left in the direction of Les Insouciantes.

The bar inside was cooling in summer and cosy in winter, and the terrace, where he settled himself, offered a premium view of the schloß. Les Insouciantes may have had one of the best locations on the square, but it had known generations of discontent, and this suited Markus, who looked to be a different colour than before. The nondescriptly pale boy had been steeped in varnish—a pale wooden carving, lighter in shade but not dissimilar to the Löwenmensch.

She felt obnoxious for sitting down without being asked, and parking herself much closer to him than she had intended, for which she received Markus's liquid eyes parked meditatively on her chest. The waiter brought a large black coffee to which he added five sugars, his eyes not once moving from her.

She was fifteen when she decided that they should sleep together. There was very little forethought and, as usual, no discussion. She wanted a lover to set around her like concrete. She wanted to melt like ice. Yes, she wanted all those kinds of things. Markus was a better person than she was, and making love with him would make her a good person, too. She unstuffed her bra. She considered shaving, and making herself into a doll down there, a baby, just so he'd pick her up and play with her. Don't be ridiculous, she thought, and did it anyway. His parents were florists with shops all over the region, and after they had sex, which happened automatically, in the way of a bodily function, he gave her flowers under the condition that she knew they hadn't been fit to sell and so hadn't cost him a thing. But she would never have questioned his manners. Her virginity was removed with the forbearance of a kindly vet.

Ute didn't expect him to speak, and Markus obliged her by removing a sketchbook from his parka and scratching away with the same pencil stub as the one favoured by Papa.

—What have you been doing this morning? she said.

Some air seemed to be leaving him. —Vineyard.

—Later?

Markus's eyes narrowed. —This.

He rasped his answer. She wanted to go to the pharmacy and get him something for his throat, for the pain.

—Tomorrow?

—Same.

Markus sucked at his teeth as he worked, as she had remembered, but he was a different artist than before. He was no longer so focused on accuracy. What she could see of the work seemed to be vaguer, and better, which was all very well, for there must have been fifty self-portraits in the sketchbook. Each one looked as though it had been finished off with a damp rag.

But what would an accurate self-portrait have looked like?

Sweat was breaking out on his top lip and pooling in his eye sockets. The heat and the parka explained the sweat—then another coffee appeared, and she began to worry about his heart as well as everything else. She considered what he'd been through to lead him to a life in the Sankt Thomas and the medication that came with it.

He caught her looking at the sketchbook. —You can have one, he said.

Ute went through the pictures, assuming the solemnity of an auditor. Markus vetoed every one she chose. At the last minute, she found one where he had drawn himself with the short, fair hair of old. His hair in the picture was wavy and she wanted to brush it and correct his mouth into a smile.

—It would be good to see you smiling, she said.

There was another drawing. He'd begun it as she'd been talking. It was quite rough, but he had filled in the veins on her temple, the ones that she had always seen as scars.

She was half afraid to say, —If it doesn't make any difference to you, do you mind if I talk?

Markus didn't have anything to say to this. He was working.

— I've always craved a child and I've always pictured myself having one with you. Mothers and fathers, loving each other with a force that would stop the river. I've always believed that. But anyone with my surname—am I the last one?—needs to think carefully about parenting. I'm used to feeling ashamed of my family. Any child we might have would surely be ashamed of me.

It was like she was trying to deceive Markus but everything she said was true. Some scars were smaller than a nail clipping, and others were as thick as a coil of rope. She had always wished hers ran all the way from the corner of her mouth to her ear in a Joker's smile. But you didn't get to choose the dimensions of your scars, and it just so happened that she lived her life in the same way as Papa had lived his—as if, simply by being born as Pfeiffers, they had done something wrong.

But, of all the things she had never told anyone, her feelings for Markus were the most private and the most inconvenient. She felt herself disappearing into something she already was.

Papa was on the bed, dreaming his open-eyed dreams: Berti; big-boned nurses; West Germany's famous team of nineteen seventy-whenever.

The stained glass set into the window—his own handiwork—shed a modest rainbow on the flagstone floor. Mama had just been over the floor with a dirty mop, upending the bedside tables so that there was an aura of a sad, brown schoolroom.

Papa's breathing was the sound of a swirling tide, his lungs working hard to process the bad nappy smell.

—Could we open a window?

—He doesn't like it.

—Is it up to him?

Theirs was a nice house, one of the most photogenic and one of the most tucked away in all of Heidelberg, and her parents should have looked after it better. And there was a piss bottle by the bed.

—Mama, can you please do something with that? It's making me, I don't know what else it's doing but it's making me nervous about everything that's going on around here.

—Why would I take it away? He likes it.

Ute chose the next thing she said carefully. —I don't understand what you mean.

—He gets a litre a day. This one is not finished yet.

There was another bottle in an open drawer Ute hadn't seen until now. She wrapped her sleeve around her hand and, asking God for a miracle, took the bottle, whose contents resembled the expulsions of a dying, dehydrated animal, and smelled it.

Oblivion came with an open bar. Schnapps.

—That's quite a lot. A litre.

—It makes him happy.

—A litre?

—Any less would just annoy him.

—But he goes to bed very drunk?

—And happy.

—So he must wake up drunk?

—I suppose that's fine, Mama said.

Her father was living someone's desert island fantasy. Good for Papa, good for him!

They got him into the bathroom, which all those years ago had shone like a morgue. By now, the existing tiles would have made it back into fashion, but they had been replaced by three-quarters of a butterscotch wall. The entire room was conspicuously butterscotch, apart from a shower cabinet whose frosted glass bore etchings of grape clusters that resembled an assemblage of dog turds. Etchings of turds on the tiles. Etchings of turds on the mirror.

There was no clear sense of where the old standing bath could have been. The original bathroom had steps going up the side, tiles running to the ceiling and their thin towels hanging—a child's idea of a ghost—from hooks which, in a preordination of a life with wet towels, were always hung too close together. Papa used to tell his racy jokes in the bath, and underscore his punchline with a wink. (Germans did know how to have fun, if they thought they could get away with it.) Every night at eight o'clock, he would announce the time and run the tap. Papa alone could immediately withstand the scalding water, and would soap himself vigorously and rinse himself so that the water that awaited Mama and Ute resembled stirred whey. Ute was sensitive to temperature so Mama would make sure the water was blood-warm and perfect before inviting her in. Some nights her mother sang, other nights she told a story until the water became too tepid for her to bear, even though Ute would have stayed in there all night. And in that brief interlude, when the bath was all hers, Ute would feel more alone than if she'd been there herself all along—for she had figured out that staying in the water was another way of delaying bedtime and prolonging the evening, when Mama was always in a better humour.

When Ute first moved in with Tort, he enjoyed the fact that she preferred them to bathe together. She would picture the standing bath with Mama and Papa in it. On trips abroad, in hotel bathrooms that couldn't accommodate the two of them in the bath at once, Tort would sit on the closed lid of the toilet with a newspaper and a room-service miniature. They would talk before he would leave her alone and, remembering that loneliness was always accompanied by excitement, she would not get out of the water until the bath had gone completely cold.

Papa shuddered when Mama grabbed for him, but she had good technique, and in seconds he was undressed and uncertainly naked before them. Lovely scabs ran all the way up his hairless shins, bruises all over his poor saggy thighs.

He cracked a sweet smile then went to take a step but evidently decided against it. There was something bold and dashing in the way he fell.

The lighting wasn't what it could have been, and he was visible first in silhouette, a bird beating its wings, suspended for a second or more in an updraft, hanging there so as to take the measure of his own grace in the falling. Ute felt herself grazed by the breeze. He was looking over at her—he might have been—and if it wasn't for the murderous look in his eyes, all of this had been ordained in the way that an Olympic high-diver makes the climb to the board before standing on it to absorb the energy of the crowd, only to vault into the air and pirouette through it and be suspended in it, before crashing straight through the swimming-pool floor, taking the tiles with him, smashing them to smithereens.

Ute was marvelling at her father suspended in the air when in a masterfully fluid change of direction he ploughed into the etched glass of the shower cabinet. The glass survived but, having broken his fall, the tiles were smeared with Papa's blood.

He looked a little chalky but he would live past today—that was her only thought. The man who used to tell dirty jokes in the bath.

His legs were scissored under him while they cleaned up the cut on his skull. Mama's look said, yes, this is an odd scene you are being presented with. But another fall might knock some sense into him, and you should not be surprised by it. If you are going to stay for the summer, you should not be surprised by anything, it'll be one thing or another, so you do your best and we'll do ours, and everything else can look after itself.

And Papa, blasted on schnapps, couldn't have given two shits.

This was the excitement of the last day on the job—a job lasting a week. There was the tang of freedom to it all, the whisper of high season, and his new handle on it, the remarkable events he might encounter. The plan was, what was the plan?

One day soon he'd turn his head to listen to the sky—a small bird he'd learn the name of—and he'd know then that the sad feelings would have passed from him. But the plan for now was to get the nose back in the books. Concentration propelled by tea from a flask, packed lunches, a tin of mackerel for the Omega-3s, some fruit, whatever was in season, sweetened by all the concentrating and thinking. He'd make it a summer of learning, little errands and wanders. There were paths to take to the Holy Mountain, as far as his good ideas would let him. He'd take into himself for a spell, there'd be an understanding with the season, they would hold onto one another. Any trouble he'd get into would have come looking for him.

In the shadow of the fiery Heiliggeistkirche sat the stately old Gutperle. Triumph in a blackboard proclaiming eight euro for a pork knuckle. Reception for the B&B was a varnished wooden sign at the back of the bar. Up the wooden staircase and Seanie Donnellan's new centre of operations was living tribute to varnish, to teak.

There was a wardrobe the size of a galleon and into it was built a cot with a thin mattress. On the ceiling, there was a trompe-l'œil illustration of a busy wedding scene. To think of the poor child bride deflowered on that three-foot bed.

Seanie took a nap in his clothes, a rapid hover over the cot. He was especially cautious about the cot, a wallower's bed.

All his life—all his life, yes—he'd've rather had the eyes out of himself before talking to a girl. He'd learn a new language rather than talk to someone at a bus stop. Psychotic thoughts, the spicy larynx, at friendly chats. What changed, and he took his time about it, was meeting someone worse at it than he was.

Hannah had appeared in his life the way people do when they've come to deliver a summons. They were down by the river after a long day and night in Les Insouciantes. She informed him that he smelled like all sorts of things, like a train platform, and that was them, home then for something approaching a scuffle on a bed as hard as a board. Nudity in Germany seemed to be a procedural matter. She set about him as if she was changing a tyre.

Seanie took himself back there, the scenes running on familiar tracks, the glamorous mornings, the falling in love part of love, the nights spent on the Neckar-side under strawberry moons and in Saturn light.

He wasn't a great man for the names of moons, but what an awful waste of love was the point. They'd tear each other asunder, but the silences were like midnight on Christmas Eve. She liked a good brood over half-nothing, and his mind would start to hasten. For it wasn't him she was interested in at all but Ireland. She was grateful for the existence of harps, the turns in tunes, and the soul following. And, it wasn't her he'd fallen in love with either, it was the town itself.

His version of love was love that took in the physical world—the mountains above the place, the clouds above the mountain. Elusive, drifting love that he couldn't always see and didn't always recognise. Clouds and winds replacing actual things. Density of weather heralding emotions that weren't separate from life but a part of it and essential to it.

He thought he might tip along to see what was what at the Pfeiffers. This was his night to deliver to Christa. The hash was their secret, the whole business beginning with a sly offer of a puff to Julius. For the shakes, the calamitous fucking shakes. This is a very bad idea, said Christa, before medicinally milling into the stash herself, medicinally liking it, and kitting herself out with a handy little pipe. She began asking about bongs then. Bongs, for the love of God.

Seanie went with solicitude to the old bridge. Dagmar was famous for the dope and she was famous in the altstadt for working on any given day at Der Braunbär, Au Tanin Agile, Tôt ou Tard, Susanna's, Geist am Himmel, Les Insouciantes, Da Marco and Die Schweinewand. She was the reason why there were no jobs in any of these bars for Seanie (son of Noel) Donnellan of Donnellan's, Cloonfad.

Dagmar palmed him a package. —Sweet Demon. Nice and mild. Go easy on the 9 Pound Hammer, I don't have much left.

A quick belt of the Sweet Demon and the options for the evening began to multiply.

Seanie made tracks via the tired old river. No news at all from the boats moored at the bottom of Marstallstraße, the boatmen had all gone beddy-byes.

Mooching up the lane, and suddenly appealing was the life of an animal turned away in its pen. The hen appeared to mutter something sarcastic. Say it to my face, hen, he thought.

It looked as if Hannah was off out (he'd have to drop in for his bags), but sitting on the steps was the Pfeiffer daughter. She was doing her breathing exercises or something.

—Howya now, he said to a tasty silence.

Not a little like Hannah, in certain ways, the blood moving slowly, and the running of the eyes over people. But this one was coming from her own eerie place entirely. She had the carefulness of a sentry, and the stance. But for the mobile phone in her hand, there was a mist of old-time sadness off her. Give her a bonnet, some embroidery.

—Is anything the matter?

—Yes.

Every word held torment. He'd seen this in her mother, often he'd see Christa pulling away, making private plans for herself. But Seanie liked the daughter, or thought he might. And, liking (that's all it had to be) offered hope, if ever you were in the market for it.

—I was just saying hello. But I could come back. I'm never far away.

—My father has had a little accident.

—Oh?

—It was with the shower stall.

—He does that all the time. He'll end up going through the wall one of these nights.

—He tried his best to.

—Is he alright?

—He will be, she said. A little like the hen.

Christa was from somewhere finding the practised tone of a surgeon. So delicate was her handiwork that only a little did she and Julius bicker. The dried blood was scoured off his forehead, a daub of schnapps applied to the wound. Nare a wince out of him either, nor any complaint at all.

Seanie was taken back to the day when he met the Pfeiffers. Not even a week in residence, Christa'd heard him cracking up. It was a day like this one, the sun bating down and a gallon of weinschorle in him and out it all flew: the bank holiday, the month's mind, Seanie in the foetal, in the hydraulics. She came down the stairs like a ton of bricks, parlaying the information with a straight face and with neighbourly tact. With the glass and all, they could hear everything and it was clear that something was upsetting him and, for that, they were very sorry. But were they able to eat their meal in peace? So could he please stop crying.

He tucked Christa's stash in behind the photo albums, thinking then to switch on the telly. In Bauamtsgaße, sadness was often indistinguishable from boredom, and there was fuck-all the Pfeiffers didn't know about boredom. He asked Ute a few more questions about herself. The answers were lucid and quite to the point.

—No.

—Yes.

—No.

—No.

—Yes.

Seanie was trying to follow a few leads, but they were soon in the vicinity of a solemn moment. In the silence, all the carry-on of the bank holiday weekend began its advances. Without any forewarning, there was another visitation from Dad.

No one said they never tore the arse out of it. On the Monday this was, the Sunday, too, and most of the Saturday. But on the Saturday morning they'd gone for a walk. Normally you had to trick Dad into going for a walk but he was the one who'd suggested it. In and of itself that was a lot to take in. On Saturdays, he shaved with water straight from the kettle (it would look like someone had skinned one of his Early Girls), but this time he was after more of a spruce-up, and it was into Tom Joyce's with them.

Dad's eyes in the mirror were vivid and mobile, and there was something pacifying about being down in the barber's chair.

—Will you listen to me if I talk?

—Go on.

—You're nothing like us. Some would say that's a good thing, but there's a fine line.

—And I'm on it? Seanie said.

—Because you've no mind of your own. I'd even go as far as to say there's a small touch of the mendicant about you. A lost soul, there's a market for them.

It was a bit early but there in the chair, Dad brought out the hipflask he kept for emergencies.

—I've had a bright idea, he said.

—We all have those, Tom Joyce said.

He was floating with the clippers. Dad had lovely ears altogether, the lobes on him like little jelly babies. The fineness and length of the neck area was not something you'd associate with a rural publican.

—You're not to listen to me anymore. All my talk about home and hearth, the trembles as you pull up the lane, there isn't an ounce of sense in it. You won't make anything of yourself in this place. Your days will be spent in very small circumferences. So go, go where we won't find you. We'll give you the head start. You have notions—so do we, we were fucking going to call you Thaddeus—and you have your languages, so you have a choice. Don't go to France. Only they know why we're not welcome. Italians'd see you coming, with your knapsack and your chinos. These are all compliments by the way. Who's left, the Germans?

—Germany, no way.

—What were we doing learning the language then?

—For the Leaving, for the points.

Dad closed his eyes and said, —One thing the Germans know is that people have it in for them. So you can get up to all sorts, go around doing heroin and having abortions, and they'll line up to congratulate you. There's people on the bus bollock naked, flaking into one another. No remarks whatsoever. Everyone going on with their packed lunches, rustling tinfoil. Oh Jesus, it's a marvellous place. Another thing is being set about by a seven-foot heptathlete. All hearsay, of course, I'm only picking up reports, but you'd be beyond yourself if you came across a hammer-thrower. Medium build so you can relax into it a bit.

—Don't, Dad.

—Why not?

—Then again.

—Then again is right.

—I went there for the carp. My God those are dark rivers and I wouldn't have been near man enough for the hills. Never mind the rivers, they're dark, it's a cruel world, but it's the people, the plumbers and the electricians. Never in your life have you seen a tidier van, tidier than any office. Nor are they much given to the niceties, which is just what you need for yourself. You could write your name on a pile of fivers and go around dropping them just for the craic of seeing them show up at home in the letterbox. They'll find you. I'm not exactly selling it am I? But there's a sweetness in the air, there's not a bit of menace in them. They've done the work and the blood runs slow. And the heptathletes, am I getting the message across at all? Go on, make your own music.

—What about Mam?

—She'd say the same but mightn't be as nice about it.

—And you?

—I'll be here when you get back.

Sure, he died then a few days later. With a nice new haircut. No baking trays were involved.

Electrified by the visitation, to the Pfeiffers, Seanie said, —Have you ever had a tomato warm from the bush?

You have. You're as well not to bother as put a tomato in the fridge. Cherry tomatoes? Don't be codding me. Big ones, like an arse cheek, that's what you're after. If that doesn't put you off your dinner. But I've seen some lads peeling tomatoes for sauce. What kind of world are we living in when people are peeling things for sauce? Eat them like apples, like the tomatoes they are. Picture my face eating one right there in the garden. It's the memories they carry, that's what I'm after here. You'll have your own memories, Julius, but I'll bet you that wartime tomatoes didn't taste any better, nor any worse necessarily, than the ones in our garden in Cloonfad. I'm not having anything other than agreement on that score. Just don't put them near the fridge. You wouldn't last long in our house doing that.

Seanie came up short. How long had he gone on? He'd the Sweet Demon to thank for that. But there was another reason for all the yap. He didn't want to leave, he didn't want to be alone.

His adoring audience: Julius taking the remote control from Christa and Ute going through the cupboards.

—C'mere, he said. I'm going on. Next time I'll give you a poisoned dart.

—If you stay for dinner, Ute said, you can tell us more about the tomatoes.

Papa insisted on the highlights of the Brazil match. Seanie had his hand and was telling him the players' names, and their clubs, and their cities' distance from Heidelberg.

—Look at their faces. Can you imagine what that's like? Humiliating someone in their own back garden, at their own barbecue. That's what this is to them. Have you ever met a Brazilian who wants to leave a party?

Football with the sound down was quite a relaxing spectacle. It all looked so beautiful on TV, the sweet grass shining under artificial light, the German team alive to their toes. But Ute had never seen a footballer embarrassed to be scoring a goal before. It was difficult for him as well as the Brazilians to take it all in. The organisation of the German team was something to see, Seanie said, the way they moved as one. He thought the first goal dropped like a chestnut from a departing crow. The others were no less momentous.

She remembered that Tort used to do that—make out that football was all very mysterious, when it was not difficult to play and less difficult to understand. There was no ambiguity about what the players were there to do. She had read about it all in the paper—another unification of Germany they were calling it: lab technicians from Mainz and bakers from Kaiserslautern, coke dealers and plumbers from Düsseldorf who shared taxis on the way from the airport and drank beers under a parasol in the downpour before kick-off. In South America, in a carpark outside the stadium, they saw themselves somehow in one another. She imagined people saying things to strangers of which they would normally be ashamed.

Papa had his head cocked to one side. Out went his hand and Mama scurried to the bedroom, reappearing with the remainder of his ration of schnapps. There was an unhealthy amount left, but down it went in one, two, three gulps. This was not a moment to look disapproving—Ute couldn't help herself—and Seanie overdid a theatrical round of applause. Mama on the other hand seemed faint, her limbs heavy. Her normally quicksilver fingers botching up the job of peeling Papa's boiled eggs.

Seanie was setting the table. This must have been what they did when Ute wasn't here. No doubt the three of them made a good team. Mama put some water on to boil, sloshing water on the floor without mopping it up.

—Papa could slip, Ute said.

Mama dropped a tea towel onto the floor, directing with her foot, all the while mouthing Ute's words back at her.

—Is there anything you want to tell me? Ute said.

—I'm busy here.

—Busy being you were smoking in the bedroom?

—Nobody asks me that question.

Mama gave the water a sniff then salted it with an exaggerated timidity that made Ute smile. She kept her thoughts to herself while Mama buried herself in the cupboard and came out with a vacuum-packed parcel of maultaschen: Ute's favourite dinner.

Seanie took control of cooking, Mama watching in devotion as he let the dumplings boil until they looked about as appetising as a mound of tumours. The Italians had finesse—as did the French, since it was their word—but, when it came to pasta and the like, didn't the Germans apply themselves as well as anyone.

—Hands up who's hungry, he said.

When Mama went to cup his chin in her hands, he said she'd had enough to smoke for one day. He was allowed to say the things Ute wasn't.

Papa meanwhile was unblinkingly sipping schnapps. Ute tested one of the plates with the back of her hand. Her father once placed celestial importance on warmed plates. They all ate, Papa demolishing his first portion before Ute had even taken up her cutlery. The pasta was overdone, as she had come to accept, but the fillings were like lava, and there can't have been any feeling left in the roof of anyone's mouth.

Whenever her father was happy, or giving the impression of it, he would rub the top of one foot with the sole of the other and he was doing something like that now. He was humming, too, and alternating between emptying Ute's plate and Mama's. For such a meticulous man, eating off someone else's plate seemed akin to scandalous behaviour. But he wasn't her papa anymore, he was someone better, and less busy, and happier. Drowsy, farting, useless, and lucky to have found a new friend.

Papa extended his hand and Seanie placed in his palm a single toothpick from a beer glass containing pens and nail files. In this house, nothing was where it should have been but everything had a place.

The plane was in its ascent, and only a small rumour of panic. He walked on out of there to a fine hum of stars and not for the first time the Neckar sending out its invitations. A crumble, just a pinch, of 9 Pound Hammer and soon he was in a nice fix for himself. He sent up a prayer for more of that breeze.

The instruments took another moment to right themselves. A thought came to him then, as if it had been cosmically percolating.

Some class of a scene was building between her and the mother, and Ute had gone to her room with nare a toodle-oo. Something was afoot in Bauamtsgaße. She was home to a fine welcome of damp tea towels and her father digging his own grave around himself.

Seanie began to chew on an idea.

Summer was a long stretch, and wasn't there a bar in Cloonfad with his name above the door? Donnellan's. Tasty black pints and the meaning of life. He'd a hankering for wet wool and drink-driving and rusty cars. Roses. The thundering bass of the wind. Messy gardens, a ridge of spuds, a gawp out over the country serene.

But it was no given thing, the publican's life, no given thing at all. Some kind of social worker and arse wiper. It paid, and it didn't. You'd be buried up to your bollocks in the Christmas drinks for the regulars, dole day, the funeral stiff ones. Bank holidays, smartly he moved on from any talk about bank holidays. For he knew all there was to know about the bare wastes of winter, summer's darling Fridays bulling into the desolation of a Monday morning. Had you a sense of humour you'd have called it religious.

The old bridge was busy at all hours of the night. There was a messy pile of young people, one of them using a collie as a pillow. Only for their sweetness, he would have had them over the wall to drown in the Neckar. But a German hippy was actually a very fine thing. He knew by them, and was reassured by them, how they crawled from season to season.

Home was just something that played on the mind, a low whistle, and he had come to think he was needed there. With the phone warm in his hand, Seanie called the only number he knew off by heart.

—Well? Mam said, then hung up. He called back.

—What was that?

—New landline, don't know the buttons. What are they saying there then?

—What are they saying about what?

—We'd know well you were a long time away. The final, will they go hard? You can't sit back against an Argentinian. I heard some guff about a stomach flu. Every last one of them with galloping runs. All types of vomiting. What are they saying about that?

—I haven't heard. They'll be well hydrated anyhow, according to you.

—It's all the positive thoughts. They're well used to a medal. The trophy cabinet in a German house, it'll be bigger than the fridge. Have you noticed that?

—I haven't come across it personally.

—I've been doing some analysis on their defence. It's a fortress. The foundations are that deep. They've a moat with skeletons floating in it. You'd be there seven days with arrows raining down on you. It's a very intense, controlled operation they're running.

His voice weakened and not for effect.

—I've something I need to say.

—Is this some kind of obscene phone call?

—What would you say if I was to come home?

—I'd ask what you'd done. Were you bold? You were. You've gone all the way this time, you've killed someone.

—I haven't killed anyone.

—You surprise me. You jumped in that river to impress someone then. I knew you would one day.

—I am down there now. And I haven't jumped in any water.

—Case in point. You might do.

—This is nothing to do with the river. Me and Hannah are, it hasn't worked out.

—Some accounts say that this might have been overdue.

—Anyhow, I'm coming home.

She inhaled down the line at him. He could see it now, her staring with violence at the air.

—Good enough for you. You've been running wild long enough. You've hit that age, haven't you? You'll be firing out children within a year.

—Who with?

—Do you have a tan?

—A small bit of one.

—You'll have the place rode so.

—That's not my intention.

—Not your sole intention. Will you bring the weather with you? I could do with a colour. I've news for you, it's getting very seasonal in this house, and I'd really like the doctor to take more of an interest in me. What else am I doing but traipsing around the town? Standing in shopping centres.

I miss you, Mam, he wanted to say.

There was Dagmar doing her final rounds. Last call for the Sweet Demon. He was tempted to sit her down for a talk (for how badly he wanted someone to talk to), but she was rotten with the heat and all the Pils she'd have drunk at work. The good promise of the afternoon had faded into spacey hand signals. But it was a hot old night, and they were all of them in one way or another overcome by it.

The town was always quiet at night. Tonight, in particular, the heat had made zombies of everyone. It was too hot for conversation, what Ute could hear was speech drying inside parched mouths. The sky was a strange colour, egg-washed pastry came to mind, and the air had a different taste than in Ireland—sweeter, less saline, and more to her liking.

Mama had been putting Papa to bed but Ute was not ready for that kind of spectacle. She decided instead to seek some breeze on the bridge, and it was there she saw Seanie smoking by the monkey statue. The river was making her drowsy and she found a spot out of his line of vision where she could watch the water roll by. She watched him walk away before taking the steps to disembark the bridge and turn right towards home.

She found herself borne along the cobbles behind him. But Ute could see where he was going and it wasn't along Neckarstraße, which was by far the most direct route to her parents' house and his. She was also worried that, not five minutes after saying goodbye, Seanie wouldn't recognise her, or, having completed his time at Bauamtsgaße and therefore unobligated to be polite he might recognise but not acknowledge her. That's the kind of thing Irish people did, pretend they didn't know you when they did.

She followed him all the way to the McDonald's by the station. A bus had stopped on the way from somewhere vague in Romania to somewhere vague in the Netherlands and the passengers had disembarked to smoke, seven of them puffing in different directions, every one of them as wary as a Comanche. It was thirty degrees but one of the women seemed to be wearing everything she owned.

Seanie was sitting in a booth and—she felt queasy at the thought—had seen off five or six cheeseburgers. It took an age for him to look her way. His movements were so sluggish that he seemed to have to force himself to move.

—Haven't you just had dinner? she said.

Seanie was eating with his mouth open, and in this she was reminded of someone. She couldn't bear to think who it might be, right down to the way he was letting the food sit there in his mouth with nothing happening. Staring straight ahead, soulfully it seemed or—oh dear—like a lummox, a combination of Tort and her father.

—I've gathered you have been supplying my mother with some goods. Do you think she's able for that stuff?

—I get her the worst I can find, if that's any consolation?

—I'd rather you didn't get her anything.

—Noted, he said, as if cutting short an unsolicited phone call.

He became absorbed in the empty pages of his book, a translation of Goethe. By the way he was making his way through it, it could as easily have been a detective novel—the last in his favourite series—and he was too impatient to wait for the denouement.

She joined Seanie in the booth. She hadn't recognised the feeling when he had said goodbye at home but certainly she felt distractable now. This was certainly not the place to be thinking about sex, there was very little of sex here, and it was beyond her—the why and how of becoming aroused in a McDonald's. Her father would probably die soon and this was what she was doing in his name. If sex was her goal, the town was full of enthralling prospects. Handsome guys: there was one, there was one; with the dumb, lucky bodies of soldiers. Nothing would have suited her better than something aimless in a vacated student dormitory. It would have been exactly as exciting and dismal as she would have expected.

—Thanks for being so good with my dad, she said.

—You still getting used to him like this?

—You could say that.

—I love hanging out with him.

—You love it?

—I don't fucking *love* it, he said.

—You love it in the way men like things.

—I enjoy his company and he seems to tolerate mine.

—I'm thinking of moving back for a while, she said. To Heidelberg.

She was off guard and in the unusual position of making the running. If she was going to be so chatty in future, she wondered if she should prepare a list of topics. Preparation was crucial and provided the kind of armour she was lacking now.

She felt something akin to relief when he said, —I was wondering where we were. Thanks for reminding me.

—It's very soft, isn't it? Compared to other places. How do you find it?

—Soft, I think.

Ute was glad, in that case, that she had found the right word for it. —I haven't made up my mind yet. I'm seeing how the summer goes.

So far, the summer had been full of surprising moments like this one. The helplessness that brought her to this McDonald's was all the more sweet and amusing because it was the last thing she would have thought of. Maureen at the paper once told Ute that there wasn't enough want in her life. What everyone needs is more desire, it gets you up in the morning. This wasn't the first time Ute had taken the wrong person at their word, but she had never known what this word meant. Want. A horde of tired travellers on their way from some place bad to somewhere worse? A tabletop of cheeseburgers? Or was it a man who'd be polite to your parents? Seanie treated her papa like an old friend—with no expectation of anything in return. There was something so decent in that, she put it down to plain decency.

A decent and—yes—charming young man she barely knew but in whom she would have placed all the trust in the world. And there was nothing with that. Here, have it: I trust you.

—It's my father I'd like to talk about, anyway. He was upset when you left.

—I'd say he's gotten over it.

—You've no idea what it's like to see him like this. Can I ask you? How are my parents doing?

One more thing about her parents. Earlier, Mama had said something out of the ordinary: I wish it were me like that, instead of your father. For your sake. He always liked life more than I did. He had more to share with you. Mama was in some kind of mourning, and was sorry for Papa in a way that seemed selfish—a testimony, Ute supposed now, to her mother's inner resolve, and as though she resented Papa for going first.

—Well, your dad is a pain in the arse. But a gentle and old pain in the arse.

—My mother?

—Like your father but less gentle.

—Would you consider spending a bit more time with him? she said.

—Can't you look after your own father yourself?

—Of course I can look after my father. As a matter of fact, I left a busy life to come here and be with him.

—You don't need my help so.

—Would you stay with him? He needs someone, and he likes you very much.

But Papa wouldn't be the problem. For such a timid woman, Mama was very opinionated. She would resist and resist and resist. It was not that she didn't like Seanie, he was her pusher, after all. Mama didn't really like anyone in her house. Ute herself was barely welcome.

—I'll pay you whatever you want, she said.

—Some form of payment would be appreciated. But I'm heading for Hahn. Thought I'd get a flight. See the homestead, check the fences.

Their relationship was perhaps two or three conversations old. Now she was going to have to get through the summer without him. Already she was missing him in every way that she could, and not even this foolishness equipped her with a single idea of where to take the conversation. Or it may have been that things were getting less complicated—with no one around her to get agitated or make her agitated, or to speak for her or over her—and that now she was in for a summer of photo albums and drives to the vineyard. All that she had come home for.

The 9 Pound Hammer was still very much at the controls. He'd been just about able to remember his manners when Ute had appeared. No bother to her that they were the manners of a seagull.

—I'll let you get on, he said.

Now she was tidying up all his cheeseburgers. He'd half a mind to see if there was an earlier bus to the airport. All the la-di-dah was going out of him, all the front.

—Is that our goodbye? she said.

—I'd be inclined to think it is. But you should know that I do love this place.

—McDonald's?

Her smile came as sudden as a squall of rain. Normally she was that touchy, and the icy dust off her. What had happened? It had to be the prospect of a summer under the same roof as her mother.

—I thought you meant this place, she said. What do you miss about home?

—Why am I going?

—What do you miss?

—I've told you about the tomatoes.

—You have.

—Tomatoes, skin and stalks and all. What I need is a bit of weather, a good belt off a storm. The tone is very windblown. And I miss it.

The way Seanie looked at the world, anything to do with parents and their children was an awful vault of sorrow. Enough of it to do you a lifetime but not enough cop to be doing anything about it. What he was actually doing was going home to his mother.

But he couldn't be sharing any of that.

—What do you make of coleslaw? he said.

As true as the houses on the hill, now Seanie Donnellan was talking to her about coleslaw.

—I don't think of it very often.

—It's big in Galway but you don't see much of it here. Not much talk of scones either. I'd do time for a brown scone. Are you a fan?

—No.

—Would you go coleslaw though?

—On a scone?

—On anything you want. Powerful stuff.

—With tea? she said

She wasn't taking him for a fool either.

—The whole nine yards. Open your lunchbox and find a scone, some coleslaw, the heart breaks with happiness.

—On the matter of coleslaw, she said. I could suggest that Germans have very nice sauerkraut.

—It fulfils many of the same functions as coleslaw, I suppose.

Then she said, —You're a lovely, strange guy.

—Lovely would have been fine on its own.

He would have offered himself there in the street outside the station, but he knew nothing of what to say of how he felt. How he wanted her to know that he wasn't running away.

—I won't keep you, he said.

It was the depths of night but he shaded his eyes with his hand.

—Do you have to go now? she said. I could suggest that we go and look at the vines.

—Bit late for grapes, he said.

Her look said beg your pardon, if you please. She raised her nose, as if to test the air.

—There's a different smell in the dark. The sap, the juice. You can feel the growth.

—Let's push on then.

There was any amount of stray bikes to be had outside the station. He felt the want of one for a crossbar as far as Neckarstraße, the two of them looking up at the friendly skies and an orchard of stars. He could always fling the bike in a hedge afterwards.

He had one old banger in mind when he saw Ute turn the other way, walking back towards town. A sudden wintry feeling when she said, —Actually, it's time to say goodnight. Perhaps we can see the vines another time? If you are ever back in Heidelberg.

He was a hopeful person, but he was inclined to think hope was not the same as optimism. For now he'd a glimmer of what it was he was leaving behind him. Not a God's notion why or how you began to know a place just at the moment of leaving it. But goodbye to these few years of it, the entire time an itchy hole from the people who were awfully nice, fastidiously polite, acutely intelligent and conscientiously gentle. The years of speak when you're spoken to, of eyes down and saying nothing to nobody.

To a row of bicycles he said, —I'll head up there anyhow, if you change your mind?

He didn't understand why he was not altogether in his being.

He was aware of his bowels.

He felt very ordinary, he felt very sick and nervous.

He felt empty and lame.

He was aware of being deprived of something.

She was nowhere in sight. Again he felt so very fucking thick. With a nice room in a guesthouse waiting for him, Seanie began the long haul up the hill.

Frankfurt Hahn was a grim old place at the best of times, so he wouldn't head off until early in the morning. Up on the hill, there'd be a woodpile for settling on for an hour. He made a joke of it in his mind, the splinters in the crack of his hole. At least the sky was dirtying over, there'd be no stars to ignore, and it would all be fine until the hour before dawn when again the clouds would clear in mockery.

Torture would come in thoughts of where she might have been going in such a hurry, and why she had come, and why she had asked him.

Could I trouble you to stay awhile?

Next time he might ask her that. These would be the first words he'd say, he'd have no trouble getting to the heart of it.

WINE WITH LUNCH

Julius remembered everything being a different colour. People were smaller in the 1930s and smelled worse and weren't as friendly as they were now. Everyone was friendly now. The exception at the time was his mother, who told Julius he was handsome and clever and destined to be someone like his father.

Later he would hear this in three sentences.

Handsome and clever.

Destined to be someone.

Like his father.

That summer, or it could have been one after, Julius met his father's new work colleagues, men with side-swept hairdos smelling of pomade made with boar fat. The little boy listened as he polished their boots to the soft, expert talk of the peas and enormous corn that would be grown the following summer, after the war, and the Spätlese wine they would make and share among themselves.

You take from the earth only what you need, plus a little extra to be safe.

Julius had no idea about the real meaning of pleasure, and what trouble his lifelong fear of it would get him into. He was glad in the end that his father would not live to see his only son get into such trouble with work and love. Life as a humble glass-maker with a workshop in the altstadt would not have made Dr Lothar Pfeiffer one bit proud. Nor would Julius ever know if Vati meant everything he said about life being better after the war.

Boarding school wasn't a hard life. It was a life without any extravagance of adjectives. It soon became his entire world, and a boy called Felix Stein became world leader.

Parentless Felix had never known otherwise, yet he called Schule Odinstal a home from home, and was self-appointed guardian to all the new entrants, many of whom came from families emptied by the war. Not much given to exaggeration in other areas, Dr Lothar Pfeiffer was described by Felix as 'an animal' and his son was duly declared as someone to be reckoned with, protected and feared. For his part, Julius never went in for all that talk of the atrocities committed by his father and his friends—gentle men who would have done no wrong.

As far as Felix Stein was concerned, it truly did not matter whether the war had been won or lost—there was botany and chemistry to be working on of an evening and of a weekend. Julius couldn't believe his friend's appetite for schoolwork, but he could believe it when Felix became so advanced in mathematics that he began tutoring their tutor.

Such reversals seemed normal when it came to the fabulous young Herr Stein.

Away from the classroom, and when he wasn't balancing equations on the dormitory wall, Felix liked to blow off steam by working on the farm next door. The land, which was owned by a young woman whose brothers had died late in the war, had seen better days, but the sandy soil was good for asparagus and the terraced hills behind the manor house were perfect for vines. Felix could work a draught horse better than anyone within miles, and Julius would accompany him as he ploughed the rows between the vines, imagining it was he and not his clever friend who was the apple of Dorothee Völker's eye. Felix, as he ploughed, modulated his snorts so they would rhyme with the horse's own.

That Julius could inform them that the Pechstein parcel was not suffering from downy but powdery mildew was immaterial to either Dorothee or Felix as they lunched together on the buttermilk and dumplings she brought to them in the vines. She always appeared smiling and suddenly, as if out of the very leaves.

Roses grew at the end of each row, and sometimes Dorothee brought with her a single flower, which Felix would never acknowledge. Julius would forevermore associate coquettish behaviour with the immortal smell of manure. Often he would see them disappear into the forest together. He would listen but not hear anything other than laughter, which he assumed was for his benefit. One day, after lunch, he followed them and came across Felix and Dorothee under an ash tree. She was covering him like a cape.

The week before they married, Christa and Julius had been invited for dinner at the Völker-Steins'. Christa wanted to know why the meal was to be at seven yet the invitation had been for three.

They had not been going out together at the time, so she had not been to the Völker-Stein wedding and had never met Dorothee. All Julius could say about her was that Dorothee had inherited thousands of acres of farmland and vineyards and was doing a good job of working with what she had been given. Julius compressed a lot into his answers, keeping it to matters agricultural.

It took them a while to reach Forst by train and bicycle, with Christa all the while wondering why they couldn't have met in Heidelberg. Weren't she and Julius the ones getting married?

They made their way along the rough paths through the vines then wheeled their bikes through the village. The Völker farm had not been damaged in the war, but nor had it seen much in the way of upkeep. Christa was busy pointing out the gaps in the fencing when she saw Dorothee waving from a tractor. She changed subject mid-sentence. Apparently Julius had not said that Dorothee was so beautiful. But the end of the harvest was in progress and Dorothee had to get the last of the Gewürztraminer to the barn for pressing. The supposed Indian summer had diverted to rain, so there was some mildew and some sorting to do of the grapes.

Christa was welcomed at the door as though she had been brought to Felix as a house-warming present. She in turn was unmoved by Felix's reasons for asking them to be there early. There had been talk of some old bottles—a Trockenbeerenauslese from Julius's birth year, the famously hot and dry summer of 1934. It was best to taste the wines in the cellar where they were stored. Christa's taste in wine and food had been formed at her mother's table, so old wine was much the same as new wine; she would be lost after the first mouthful. Wine was boring to Christa. It was nothing more than a means to being drunk, and she didn't like to be drunk. Nor had she gotten dressed up to spend the afternoon underground, and she wondered why they couldn't drink the wine in a warm, clean kitchen.

At Schule Odinstal, where he was the youngest ever headmaster, Felix was only ever Herr Stein. But he was a schoolteacher who everyone guessed was destined for greater things. At a glance, in his work attire, he was biding his time until destiny caught up with him, but for the time being he was interested in micro-processing—he had been the first man in Germany to own a hand-held calculator—and only in wine as a hobby. Farming he did for the exercise. This he explained as he led them down the wooden stairs into the cellar's tasting room, dug deep into the cliff behind the house. Most of the caves were occupied by wine sleeping in old barrels, some of them older than the house and as big as boats, and many of them reachable only by stepladders and vertiginous walkways. The mould-caked walls had Hungarian and Austrian coins stuck into them—mementos from long-departed cellar hands—but the floors were dry and hay-strewn; Dorothee had until recently wintered the cows in there. Christa was less interested in the barrels than in the hay feeder that had been carved into the rock. It would be a good manger for a baby.

Felix had lit candles and arranged glasses on the ledge of a barrel along with a half bottle of the 1934 Jesuitengarten Trockenbeerenauslese, the Völker family's first vintage. A wine so rare that Julius had never thought it might exist in real life. It wasn't Christa's idea of a pre-dinner drink, and she reprised her stated intention to go upstairs. They hadn't even been given a tour of the house.

Felix was as sure of himself as anyone Julius had ever met, but he had never come across Christa when she was at sixes and sevens.

—You can't leave without tasting, he said.

—Let's taste then.

—I will try it first. Not out of discourtesy but as a formality.

—Shouldn't you wait for Dorothee? Christa said.

—My wife is not to be rushed.

—If the wine is so bloody special?

—It's her family wine. She knows it well enough.

The Riesling was as molten and delicate as he had read and Felix had promised, but, as much as Julius was in thrall to it, he did not have the vocabulary to describe the wine in anything like those terms. His way of looking at wine was connected to Vati, and was born from duty to the parcel of vines he had inherited. Indeed, the candlelight and the striped light entering the cellar via a vault gave this the air of a solstice gathering, and took Julius into daydreams that were all his own and not his own. He was overwhelmed in the presence of all this breathing treasure. There was the cabin on the Philosophers' Walk but this claustrophobic ruin of the Völker-Steins' was everything he wanted and couldn't have. Felix's hobby was how Julius wanted to pass his workdays and spend his life.

Julius knew that the thundering sound of someone coming down the steps wasn't Dorothee. The maid said the table was set for dinner in the garden. Christa handed the glass of Trockenbeerenauslese that she hadn't tasted to Felix. She would wait for them upstairs, like a civilised person.

She came at him sideways in the dark. A stern goddess in wool trousers patched from knee to seat. She took the bottle—her family's wine—and, as though it belonged to Julius, poured herself some before raising the glass in his direction.

—To your wedding, Dorothee said.

Ever the gentleman, Felix had escorted Christa upstairs and to the patio. Julius was trying not to think of them conversing somewhere above his head. He was sure that Felix followed Christa not out of chivalry but so he could persuade her of the integrity of the basalt soils on the Völker land. As far as Julius was concerned, the fact that Felix had already found his way into Dorothee Völker's bedroom meant he could persuade anyone of anything. Christa was well capable of engaging with anyone on any subject, be it triage or blood transfusions, and well capable of making it understood that being a nurse did not mean she could be talked down to by a schoolteacher. Julius wished her well, but didn't fancy her chances with Felix, of whose charm it was said he could talk wine out of a stoppered bottle while having filed a patent for the bottle closure and moulded the glass and, of course, made the wine.

Dorothee began to move away from Julius, out of the candlelight and into shadows. It was how he imagined a ghost would float. Ghosts could play with you, too, and vanish just as soon as they had come into view, in their own time and at their own speed. Julius followed her into a neighbouring chamber housing more magnificent barrels, before she took a turn into a narrow passage at the end of which was an archway at chest height. She knew these caves well enough to guide him in darkness, bending fascinatingly at the waist before disappearing into the arch without asking him to follow.

The arches led to a cave housing the Völkers' private collection. Dorothee's parents had been Sauternes fanatics, and there were multiples of Yquem going all the way back to the comet vintage of 1861.

—We have not seen many comets lately, she said.

—Superstition.

—Even so.

—Even so.

Julius's eyes were drawn to the wall. A recess housed no more than a dozen dusty bottles whose labels had rotted to almost nothing. He understood this to be significant: not the cobwebs stringing from bottle to bottle, which were going to stay exactly where they were, but his presence here among them. There was about this room a holiness that he sensed was embodied in Dorothee herself.

Julius could hardly see her, but could feel her warm autumn aura and smell the wine's sharp honey on her breath. Everything about her presence danced around the cellar's damp.

—This is more of the 1934.

—My birth year.

—Felix said.

Dorothee said her husband's name in a way that made his presence upstairs seem inconsequential. Julius was himself oblivious to any thoughts of Christa and dinner. What was the point in dinner now?

—If they are well cared for those wines can last forever, she said.

—How patient are you?

—Not patient at all.

—We should save the rest of it for them upstairs, Julius said.

—Felix drinks it all the time.

—The 1934?

—Nothing but the best.

He wanted to taste the wine that had been in Dorothee's mouth. Her kiss was as limpid as spring water and had nothing to do with a life in which, on this day next week, he would be married.

For many years, he would consider that Dorothee had not come downstairs for a lecture on the longevity of Jesuitengarten wines. Even now, wine seemed to have little to do with what was passing between them; the ecstasy and anxiety of a prison visit you want to be over so that confinement can resume. A life without love was not without its appeal. Was love going to sweep the stairs, tally the books? Would it plant new stakes at the vineyard? He feared he would never know. The cellar would keep its secrets. Julius needed the safety of a clean kitchen, a breezy garden, Christa—because if even wine now was irrelevant, what else was?

Perhaps it was in imitation of Felix's chauffeur that Dorothee was such a courtly driver. Every gesture, whether it was indicating or turning the dial on the radio, was smooth and protected and contained just the right amount of pomp. Nothing about this woman was plain, but the enjoyment she took in something as simple as a motor car was impossible to disguise, not that she ever tried.

Julius didn't like to work, but he liked having worked, thus his weekends were hardly any different from the days surrounding them. He liked less and less being away from home. This Saturday in particular, one in which he would wake up not at home but at the Aurelia of the Waters hotel, was not only unusual but very unsettling. He had always thought this to be a toy town, a play town. Who among the Badeners did any work? None that he could see. But he had been looking forward to this weekend away for months, since long before Ute had been born. On the other hand, he had not been looking forward to a night in a hotel. Would he feel watched? Or was it that, clueless as he was about the sights and sounds of wealth, the latter as inaudible as the engine in Dorothee's new car, he was anticipating a lot of flimflam? Was it that he was intimidated by the rigid flags on the bonnet of the car that preceded them up the driveway? Or, was it that he was simply troubled by the cost? One night's full board came to the same as a week's turnover at the glass-maker.

As soon as they were out of the car—someone just took it away from them—Julius wanted to go for the dinner, which was included in their package, and would be over in forty minutes. Dorothee explained a few things to him. They would be going straight to their room without anything to eat. A drink at most and then bed. They could have dinner any other night of the week.

Julius went as far as putting his foot down about it. But Dorothee, whose wishes overrode everything else, even plans and logic, said no to the offer of a three-course meal. Julius was only able to forget the cost of dinner—for which he had paid over the odds and in advance—when they fucked until Dorothee's hair was damp and straggly. During sex she was a madwoman, instructing him to call her names and sniff her arse. It wasn't her fault to be a provoker of all that was shameful in him—it was the primary reason why he was here at all—but it was not to be put into words.

—I want you to turn me inside out. I want you to eat me like a steak. My blood in your mouth.

It was perfectly above board to talk about love, but Julius had no gift for racy talk. Afterwards she flung open the windows without paying attention to what was outside. It was summer here—as it was at home, an hour up the road—but they had not gotten to see any of the attractions as Julius had thought they would. He was excited by the thought of a hotel breakfast, anticipating the array of an afternoon tea but heartier. Toast in racks, the eye drawn to the variety, bacon prepared the American way. Of course, a boiled egg or two, and perhaps there would be some to take home.

Dorothee had not packed any nightwear. And she was fascinated by his chickenpox scars, something Christa in all their years together had never mentioned.

—Quite honestly, some of the most charming things I've ever seen.

Accustomed as he was to living with a woman who was always careful with herself, nothing on earth could convince him that Dorothee had not been sent from the bowels of the earth.

—This is a long way from Schule Odinstal, she said.

—I'm glad.

—You loved me even then, didn't you?

—You were perfect, he said. I'd have given anything for you to marry me.

—Do you remember one night you promised me just that? You promised me the entire Philosophers' Walk, the entire mountain.

—I don't remember. But I would have promised you anything.

—And what else?

—What else would you have liked?

—Would you have promised me the river?

—I'd have promised you the river.

This came out in a whisper as they were falling asleep, from one lover to another. But it was impossible to tell the truth about what was in his heart—all that cryptic stuff he left to other people—and this was a sign that Julius had been reaching for and not finding the right words. No, that was not fair. He had been very specific in the usage. But the more he considered it, the more ridiculous it became. It was precisely the absence of any promise-making in his life that allowed him to sleep every night.

Depending on what was on the books, he liked to have had breakfast and be downstairs by six—or earlier in the summer—so, on a morning away from home, it was a challenge to wait until the hotel's anointed breakfast time. Seven in the goddamn morning. These people had obviously never worked for a living.

Dorothee was an early riser, too, or so she had said. Since when did farmers—or land-owners, since that was really what she was—sleep past dawn? But Julius knew not to wake her with a kiss, which is what he wanted to do. He made as if he was sleepy for a while. She was impervious to the rolling mattress then to the folding of the shutters. Julius's repeated flushing of the toilet with the bathroom door open only served to aggravate him without waking her. He ran a bath but didn't get into it. And the smell of her, even from his seat by the window, was—he wouldn't put it into words.

Christa never liked to mention Dorothee by name, although once in the heat of a disagreement he had been called her lapdog. But even lapdogs needed their breakfast, and when Dorothee awoke he was waiting with a glass of water for which he'd let the tap run cold. He was eager to make up for lost time in the dining room.

—It's past nine o'clock.

—The hotel was kind enough to provide us with a clock.

—Breakfast finishes in half an hour. Less.

—We'll get something later, she said.

—Better a sparrow in the hand than a dove on the roof, he said.

Dorothee was the kind of woman for whom meal timetables, and mornings, held little fascination.

—I'm sure it'll be up to scratch, he said.

—Of that we have no doubt.

—Although I'm quite particular about my boiled eggs. And I will be able to tell if the coffee pot hasn't been warmed in advance.

—Why do you put yourself in the path of things you won't enjoy? If hotels put such a stress on you.

—It's no stress to want the thing you have paid for.

—Why do you always have to be so careful?

—Not always, he said. I'm here, aren't I?

—And you're making such heavy work of it.

The first thing Dorothee had ever remarked upon at school was Julius's appetite for work, so why was she going on about it now? She was one to talk anyway, being married to the fabulous Felix Stein. This was a remark Julius might have made out loud, but outside of their lovemaking spelling things out was one of the things he and Dorothee did not do. Spelling things out would only lead in one direction. He had, for instance, an ingrown toenail. He wasn't about to share that with her, was he?

Dorothee took a pillow from his side of the bed and put it under herself. Was she expecting to be brought breakfast, lunch and dinner in this position? This was not the point. It was now a matter of conscience or, rather, one for the soul. They had missed dinner and now they were going to miss breakfast, which he could not conceive of.

He could have made life easier for himself by having an affair with someone of lower standing than Dorothee, or of lower standing than himself, although it was awful to think that he already had one of those. And what if anything was the matter with Christa as a mother? Once upon a time he had envied her ignorance, now it was her willingness to accept the affair with Dorothee that troubled him. He would go home to her tonight, the weekend having served its purpose, and have no power left to provide for her. Tonight, towards his family Julius would behave like a visiting diplomat. Gifts would be presented tactically, in exchange for affection.

He could at all times—even in her absence, especially then—feel Christa's mockery. And now Dorothee was at it too.

—If you're so desperate for your boiled eggs, we can ask them to send some up.

—After half nine?

—Yes, after half nine.

The teasing went on all morning. But Dorothee, after some persuasion, deigned to visit the dining room for lunch, where the other diners were dressed, the women as well as the men, in polo shirts and white flannels. The wearing of Julius's only suit had conveyed a misunderstanding of the dress codes so overwhelming that it would have probably been better to walk into the dining room naked. Dorothee was wearing what she always wore, and didn't seem to care that Julius was dressed like one of the staff. He wondered then if Felix Stein had ever worn the wrong thing to eat a meal.

To think that a few minutes prior—until seven minutes after nominated check out—he had cradled Dorothee Völker-Stein in his arms. He would have stayed upstairs, too, but she had teased him about his timekeeping, and he hadn't been sure how to respond.

There was a pleasure in ordering a Völker Riesling from the middle of the list—this was the thing to do—and he felt he could do it because it wasn't his wine. He would never have ordered his own wine in a restaurant, mind you. But his wine was not available in any restaurants. Julius flinched when the waiter with too much fanfare poured an inch of wine into his glass. He thought of all the ways he could have shown respect by offering Dorothee's own wine to her to taste. Then he swirled the wine and smelled it without tasting—the right thing to do—before pronouncing it fit for purpose.

—Delicious? Dorothee said, before asking the waiter for the cork.

She tasted the wine with her hands flat on the table. Her beautiful hands with the turquoise stone on each index finger, the hands that had been on him. If it wasn't for the other parts of her, chief among them the most decorative of arseholes, Julius would have loved her hands the most. As far as he was concerned, the jewellery was unnecessary.

—Do you really think it's delicious?

—Of course, he said. It's yours.

Was it mere bad luck that Julius hadn't detected the cork taint in the wine? —It's very faint, she said. But it's there.

—You should know.

—Perhaps you should taste it one more time, she said. Wine should be nothing more than sweet water. This is like something out of the river. Not a polluted river, but brackish. Now, if we were at home I might even have them cook with it. But since I suppose they know who I am, I have to send it back.

He looked at the window, not out of it but at it. A fine summer rain was falling and disturbing his enjoyment of the smooth glass. When it came to wine, Julius Pfeiffer was the sort of person whose destiny it was to be habitually a little bit in the wrong. Those who knew wine really knew it but he knew glass and loved it. His lot in life was to love the sureness of a glass more than what was in it.

He wondered aloud if he should order a bottle of something else and if so what? A basic champagne would have been a good gesture and hardly more expensive than the Völker wine.

—We are fine with water, don't you think? Dorothee said. There is always more wine.

Their starters arrived, and to see Dorothee with a mouthful of pike gave him a blush of envy for the fish. He was shocked that her buoyant mood had not been affected by the below-par bottle. His soup annoyed him. On they went without him eating, in spite of all the goings-on among the waiters between courses. Uneasily at first, he reached for Dorothee's hand. She allowed him to take the one she wasn't using to smoke. Women smoking, he felt very ahead of the times, and worried less about his outfit and that soon he'd be signing for the bill.

Dorothee's easy way of drinking the water they had been left with was so enchanting that, before Julius could raise a glass of it to toast their lovers' weekend, he had almost forgotten about his mistake.

—I'm telling you, he said. You know how to live.

—This is only the half of it.

—What else is there?

—What else is there? Let me see, I might suggest some Völker Riesling. Do you think they have any?

He was being teased again. He responded in the only way he knew how, which was to be lost to the window. The hotel grounds looked ever more luxuriant after the burst of rain. Although Dorothee was right in front of him, Julius went out of his way to picture them together outside, one of them coyly referencing the breeze-swept sexuality of the honeysuckle (silly bush, bad bush), the other remarking on the smell of summer, whatever that was. But there was nothing of life in this scene, and certainly no emotion in it, precisely because it was behind glass.

It was so much easier to fantasise about Dorothee than to be across the table from her. At that very moment, being there involved watching her lick the gravy off her knife—something about her pleasure in it suggesting she was an easy-to-please orphan instead of who she really was: the better, reckless part of his soul, the out-of-body part of him that didn't care about breakfast times or corked wine. It went against everything he knew, but Julius began to lick gravy off his knife too. He did it without thinking, only really coming to when they were being served coffee. Once Dorothee had eulogised the sugar lumps it was time to pay and go. He decided against asking if their breakfast entitlement would be valid for lunch.

PART TWO

The Counter-Reformation

The finest of evenings for a poetical notion. Metaphysically speaking, a night under the stars would always stand to you. The benches of the Philosophers' Garden were sun-warm and he lodged himself on the shrivelled wood, his face for a languid minute or two in the hydrangeas.

He'd gone as far as Hahn, and checking in for the flight. He'd gone as far as walking up the steps of the plane.

He got on the phone to Mam.

—I'm not myself, he said. I just don't know what I'm at.

—Don't know what you're at is right, she said.

This being just one of the many insults the world would put to her that day. She was down a husband, and now prayers would have to be ordered for a son on walkabout. Her general suspicions would have been confirmed: the arse was out of Seanie Donnellan's trousers and, in the seat of a plane, he was having a small freak-out for himself, the uselessness getting very heavy in him.

What do you do but drill on in to the quiet of yourself, the grinding thoughts?

He was guided up out of the seat and to the doors as they were closing. They weren't going to let him away at first.

—It's a bit stuffy in here, he said. I have a message to run.

What was that now, a rat gnawing on his toes? Hadn't there been a strangling in the forest? Someone asleep on a bench was one fine way to catch the eye. Swiftly Seanie rose from the bench and with thrust-back shoulders got himself along the path and over the wall to the safety of Julius's vineyard.

There had to be something of yore in sleeping among the leaves. A philosopher's nap in amongst the frogs, waking up with a head full of earwigs.

The town was in the same place as the last time he'd looked, but it wasn't for the uplifting views he'd taken to the hills. As Ute had promised it might, the vineyard light was thickening about him. The smell rising up from the soil and the wholesome hill smouldering in its rest.

The question arose: in the morning, would Seanie just show his face at Bauamtsgaße? Saying nothing to no one. Ute had wanted him to do what exactly? How long would they be at it? A day, a week, was there a month of work in it?

The clouds were astir and at sundown the sensation of a camera's flash signified lightning. The sky was bawling and with the rain came an attempt to limit the thinking—there'd been a quare amount of sad and frightening thinking the last couple of days. At least the weather played fair here, firing down on top of you instead of coming in from the side. He settled down to sleep under the cover of vine leaves. He lay on his front and with cheek against forearm said his prayers to the air.

The hill breathed with him and he resolved to pass the night in the company of love, the love that did its work whether it was asked to or not and was alive in Seanie still. And love's way in the end was the shelter of the mountain.

Sometime in the night, he dreamed of an animal thrashing through the vines. Standing there was a man with one giant dreadlock. The courteous way in which the vine leaf was picked from Seanie's mouth.

Mama was up and dressed. Sometimes they looked alike but not this morning—it had been a hot, damp night and Ute's hair was wet while her mother's blouse was starched and the skirt she had found looked new even though it could have been fifty years old. Her cardigan was adorned with a silver pin and her posture was of someone awaiting cross-examination.

Clothes used to matter to Mama. One Saturday in Galeria Kaufhof, Ute had tried on some lace-edged leggings that looked like something Madonna would have worn. That Mama was absorbed in shirts for Papa didn't prevent her from shooting an annihilating glance—she was suffering at the sight of the leggings—and Ute replaced them neatly on their hanger. Mama then bought herself a beret, which she wouldn't let Ute wear. That was the thing with berets, they stretched easily.

You could always count on a metre of sun this early in the morning and Mama was occupying it with her chin raised. The interlude was all hers. Ute let herself think that Mama, stoned or not, was at peace in the mornings. But she wished her mother wouldn't make so many boiled eggs. Ute had been living in Ireland and didn't eat a proper breakfast anymore. The Irish were too sophisticated for breakfast nowadays, and so busy, and keen to tell you so.

Even Tort, who bled money, baulked at spending five euro for a coffee when it was as good and as easy to have one at home.

Mama had amassed a small hill of eggshells. She tapped another egg off the table, peeled it in one hand and ate it in one mouthful. There were eight eggs remaining if Ute wanted to practise.

—How many eggs do you eat every day?

—I don't know.

—Has Dr Reuter tested your cholesterol lately?

—I would not let that woman near my cholesterol. It's as if you don't know how to peel eggs anymore.

If Ute had checked into a hotel instead she could have avoided an exchange like this. Once upon a time she would have come up with an excuse like—'Mama, I don't want to put you out.' And there was always the privacy and supposed illicitness afforded by hotels: concierges who would do anything without saying anything. Euphemism, euphemism, euphemism for the not wanting to stay with the people who didn't want you there in the first place, a category that Ute assumed included her parents.

At least Ute had packed the same tea she took everywhere, the rooibos, which was her mother's favourite.

—This is your tea? Mama said. You brought it with you from Ireland?

—Yes.

—There are shops here.

—I like to carry familiar things when I travel.

—It's my favourite tea.

—I know it is.

—Quite nice.

—That's why I buy it. It reminds me of you.

Perhaps, between the 'your tea' and the 'quite nice', all had not been lost. Mama had enjoyed something and had said so. You couldn't turn your back on this woman for a minute. There were several ways to go with this one and, somewhere along the way, hadn't Ute vowed to be kind to her mother?

—Your father is someone else's responsibility now, said Mama so suddenly that Ute was shocked into butterflying about with no apparent sense of purpose. She half-committed to peeling a boiled egg.

—What do you mean?

—He's not mine any more. I made that decision a long time ago. I want to tell you why. Let's go for a walk.

—You're not dressed for a walk.

—We're not going far.

Overnight the yard had become an avid uproar of dandelions. The unofficial salad garden had flourished, and the leaves looked chewy and smelled of—Ireland, as it happened, a meadow. New nettles were appearing before Ute's eyes. Alliums and sage as well as inedible hornbeam and lindens and butterfly-approved milkweed. There was sorrel, too, she tasted some. All the delicious rabbit food that Tort liked her to grow in the kitchen garden at The Hide.

It was declared a beautiful morning for a walk. Even though she must have been up half the night waiting to go, the thought seemed to be just occurring to Mama.

—Let's go to the river. Yes, let's.

For once Ute couldn't see the Berti stones. She felt a responsibility to the place now and would deal with the weeds later. There in the yard was a woman collecting eggs from the coop. Four eggs. Two for her, two for someone else. Ute found this Hannah person to have the countenance and the frown of a school dinner lady. Most of the time Ute was grateful for her ability to tan quickly and without burning; unlike their neighbour, who resembled the lid of a pie. And the small mercy was that Hannah did not seem to be a mind reader.

She moved towards her front door, the old workshop, and had to manoeuvre the eggs in order to reach the door handle. Ute waited until it was just too late before she offered to help so that in the end Hannah had to open the door on her own. She held out her arms so that Ute and her mother could help themselves to an egg. One each.

They all laughed together—with their lucky hen-warm eggs—and Hannah went inside and that was it.

Ute found herself to be disappointed. She had wanted the stand-off to continue. She had so many questions for Hannah. And when was the last time she'd had a really fresh egg?

It took them all of thirty seconds to reach the Neckar and another lovely and anonymous morning by the river. The water was up, like she was up.

There was a benign sky but the river was the colour of peanut butter—residue from last night's storm—and the banks were bloodied and scummy in places. On the pontoon, some Japanese tourists waited in tender silence to board one of the new cruisers. The fleet these days was so sleek that it could probably have taken the country to war if one had been in the offing. The cruisers left early and late so the water was kept free for the barges that mooched along with their cargoes of new coal and old metal. The rowers would have to chance their luck, she supposed, but Ute didn't see much activity at the rowing club this morning.

—Perhaps Papa would like an egg for breakfast? she said.

—Not likely.

—Schnapps?

—A little, yes. Why not?

They had just sat down on the steps that led down to the Sankt Hedwig. The avalanche of mansions and new residences across the river had been such a shock to Ute on the morning she arrived home. She concluded that one day she would cross the river to live on the Neuenheim side, in order to look down on the altstadt where she had grown up. Perhaps she could get planning to build something on Papa's vineyard, an ice-cream wafer like The Hide.

—When is your husband going to be joining you?

—He's not my husband.

—Does that mean he's not coming?

—I don't know. But it means we never intended to marry. And he's not here. I am taking this summer for myself. And to be with you and Papa.

—Why would you want to do that?

Mama cracked her knuckles and resumed her courtroom posture. There was a reason why she had dressed up this morning.

—Where are we going?

—We're here, Mama said. Sankt Hedwig.

Mama placed a lozenge tin containing two small joints on her lap and lit up briskly. It pleased Ute to see how ineptly her mother inhaled, no better than a child pretending to smoke with a pen. Ute hadn't smoked a joint in a few years. Tort went through bursts, as he went through phases of brandy for breakfast, but she could take it or leave it. The smoke she inhaled now made her brain feel liquid and her limbs leaden. She had no idea if this was the desired effect.

Mama took the joint from her and jabbed it in her mouth.

Ute found that—with no Papa, and no house to worry about and in which to feel uncomfortable—she felt an ease with her mother she had not felt in a long time. The river, and probably the dope, provided a sense of tranquillity which they had been incapable of providing on their own. Mama had perfected the appropriate blissful demeanour, her eyes skimming their backdrop, the river, which was effervescent with momentousness. Papa's vines were barely visible across the river, indistinguishable as they'd always been from wild scrub on a forgotten hillside.

Ute took another puff of Mama's joint—her last—then couldn't stop herself babbling: telling Mama about Tort, and about Seanie, and how they seemed alike in so many ways.

It seemed to her that once upon a time Tort had just resolved to be charming. The habit was a long time in the forming, and practised in meetings, on walks along Dún Laoghaire pier, in the queues for taxis at foreign airports; he had all the time in the world to offer lights for cigarettes to strangers, and to stand them rounds, and ask about their families. Only last month she'd seen him stand forlorn in the lobby of their hotel in Sydney, watching potential targets check out and move on with their lives and out of his. It was another of the lessons life had for her in the shape of this big brute who smacked his lips as he helped himself to a stranger's sandwich. Ute was not sure she was immune to it either. The appearance of charm was charm itself.

The first time Tort had seen her name in print—the fuss he made of it, stopping people in the street to instruct them to buy that day's paper. And the celebration dinner where the only words she said were to the waiter, and where his speech of congratulations felt to her like words of consolation. She wouldn't co-operate, she was unable to, and in the face of all this the charm kept flowing. Charm was a transferable virtue, was it not? As was generosity, as was kindness. She had continued speaking long beyond the point where her mother had stopped listening.

—What do you think it was like to live with your father? Mama said. We have been married for forty-two years. You can add to that all the time we knew each other as children. So I have known your father for fifty years, which is most of my life. And if you think I made it easy for him you're very wrong.

—I can't see you making it easy for anyone, Ute said.

—You understand me then. Do you know what I wanted to be when I grew up?

—A nurse, Mama. I know this.

The traffic on the river was getting busier. An empty coal barge registered in Liechtenstein thundered past a police boat investigating a suspicious-looking log.

—I became a nurse, that's what I was, but I wanted to be a doctor. A lot of people did after the war. It was not a glamorous job but it was useful, and I thought it was glamorous too. We had no money, no connections. So much success was about to whom you were related, and I wasn't your father, I wasn't related to anyone like a famous surgeon. But if you were to show me a map I would still be able to highlight all the clinics and every single hospital in south Germany. There was another problem. I didn't work hard enough at school, at my chemistry and biology. Doctor Christa Sönke? I was dreaming. It took quite a while to dawn on me that I was dreaming. The University Hospital needed people, and I applied and I got in. It took me a while to realise that's what I was actually doing. That I was studying to become a nurse. This was just after I agreed to go out with your father. He was persistent. And he wanted what he couldn't have—I'll get on to more of that in a minute. But it was a good hospital and there were students there from Frankfurt and Stuttgart. They were all happy to be there and eventually I was happy. The patients liked me and I liked them much better than I had expected to. It was quiet in the end, the war was long over with. So I could focus on your father, and you. Mainly your father. He wanted to be a winemaker. Even though he never said as much, I think it was important for him to escape anything to do with Lothar Pfeiffer.

Ute had always sensed herself getting prickly when others spoke of their grandparents and had been glad to reach an age, around twenty, when that generation started to die off. Mama always referred to her father-in-law by his full name. Ute's grandfather was well known, of course, but there were a lot of absentee grandparents when she was growing up and it had always been put to her by Papa that Lothar Pfeiffer hadn't been in the wrong so much as he was a doctor doing his work.

—But there was no wine after the war, Mama said. The Mosel was bombed, and the Pfalz wasn't that much healthier. There was no one to work the land anyway. I had no interest in it. But I knew that wine would come back one day and that he should be patient. I wanted him to focus on doing what he loved. Do you understand what I'm saying? I'm saying that I didn't become what I wanted, I became something else and it was better. It didn't matter for me, but for your father it did matter. He knew Felix Stein from boarding school. You know the kind of bonds you form at those places. Dorothee Völker was salvaging her family's parcels and Felix was able to save to purchase more. It was a good time to begin anyway. Vines like stress and, believe me, there was plenty of stress in the land. Felix and Dorothee would have been happy to have your father onboard. This was because of Lothar Pfeiffer of course. He was a fearsome man with a fearsome reputation and Felix Stein was exactly the kind of man to be impressed by that. A lot of people didn't want to employ your father because of Lothar Pfeiffer.

Ute had her face in her hands. Today had become about something other than Seanie. She had only ever been told what Papa wanted her to know about her grandfather, who had been an expert at holidays, apparently. Papa liked to recall the summer when he got to meet the Führer at his Berghof in Bavaria. Hitler napping in a chair had always been one of his most precious memories, although disputed by Mama, who had reminded him that he would have been two years old at the time and thus would not have remembered a thing. Ute felt bad for all that too, because Papa must have loved his father.

Mama was in a trance. She began to say something else but became distracted by a van pulling up on the dock beside the Sankt Hedwig. In as much time as it would take to snap your fingers, she flipped the joint into the water.

The driver wheeled a trolley down the gangway and deposited a case of wine and some water on board before moving off.

—Glass work is good work, engraving and etching, but from the first day it was unbearable for your father and for me. He was a success. Not overnight, but he got his own place eventually and we could buy our house. Glass work is not an art anymore, those days are gone. Your father spent more time than he wanted to making shower units and splashbacks. Of course, it wasn't wine. But he could develop all that. I think it was the only vineyard in the city at the time. Can you imagine growing grapes within view of the schloß? Do you know how difficult it is to get hold of land up there? You don't just walk up and buy land above on the Philosophers' Walk. Your grandfather again, of course. This we know. Papa had his rows of vines. Felix Stein wrote to him to say that he admired the bottle your father sent him and once more to invite your father to work with him on the Völker land. They were looking to expand beyond Forst and there were some good hills in Wachenheim. Interesting aspects. South-east facing. But it was not your father's land, so he didn't want it. Your father could not have Felix Stein's land and money, so he did not want anything. Of course, things went on after that. When he could not have Felix Stein's wine, he took his wife.

Ute could remember the first time Dorothee Völker came to their house. Tall and dark and benevolent, the first thing she did was compliment everything: the furniture, the lights and the curtains. Then she asked for a gin and tonic. Mama had no gin, or tonic, but said that she could get some. Dorothee wouldn't hear of it, she was just there to deliver some meat that Felix had set aside for Julius. Every year after the harvest and the first pressing of the grapes, Felix would get the men to scatter the lees in the forest for the wild pigs to eat. Agriculture had its limitations like anything else. The flavour of the boar was impossible to replicate in a farming situation.

Dorothee did not seem like a self-effacing person, and the conversation about the meat's virtues was very prolonged, which gave Ute the opportunity to study this woman. She was all in white even though it was halfway through autumn. And she made such a meal of the word 'wild'.

She was a toucher. Berti, Mama, everything and everyone got caressed. Ute herself saw to it that she got within stroking range—her first bewitching. Dorothee's slender wrists were often weighed down by the Native American jewellery Felix bought for her in Santa Fe. Later on, once they had employed a full-time winemaker, she opened an atelier on Dreikönigstraße, selling Tahitian and Japanese pearls and Zuni bracelets and chokers. As if to emphasise her exotic value, she opened only for a couple of hours every other Saturday.

Ute knew the opening times and would always find a reason to walk past without ever going in. On the day she was asked inside, Ute was petrified, and in talking about fashion and art and music with someone from outside the family, felt compelled to exaggerate her experience. She had never been outside of Germany, yet professed to have heard *Madama Butterfly* at the Théâtre antique d'Orange in Provence.

Dorothee spoke of Papa's vineyard, comparing the wines from his little acre to the ones fashioned by her newest winemaker, who had come from Leflaive in Montrachet. She went into the kitchen—the atelier was bigger than Papa's workshop—and poured Ute a small glass of the Völker Riesling from their Ungeheuer vineyard.

—Your father's favourite, she said.

—Papa makes his own wine, Ute said.

—When all the elements of a wine are present in the correct proportions and working in absolute harmony there is absolutely nothing you can say other than experience it and be happy that perfection exists.

Ute had carried those words with her ever since, embellishing them to the point of adage.

Dorothee opened a drawer and produced a pair of pearls, about which the same statement seemed to apply.

With an expensive sigh, she said, —Akoya pearls are also too beautiful to describe. To the untrained eye, they appear similar to freshwater pearls. But they tend to be rounder and smoother. More lustrous. Notice how cold and gritty these feel. That is a very, very good sign. Anyway, pearls are for sophisticated girls. To you, from me.

Ute was stunned and wary and excited as well as worried what her mother would say. True, when she entered the kitchen at Bauamtsgaße, wearing the pearls and the straightest face she could muster, Mama to her credit handled the taking of offence very efficiently. She got straight on the phone to Dorothee.

Ute only heard one side of the conversations, her mother's.

—The pearls are beautiful, Dorothee. Quite, quite beautiful. But you missed one simple point. You are supposed to ask a girl's mother before presenting her with something so significant. You are forcing me to be impolite, something I have no wish to be. There is a difference, Dorothee. There is a difference and you know it. I don't care if you are embarrassed—you should be embarrassed. Pearls, for Ute? I've never heard something so ridiculous. What next? Would you like to buy her a car, a house? Better that she doesn't return them herself. I will ask Julius to deliver them to the Sankt Hedwig next time they are open, whenever that is.

The pearls were long gone. But one Christmas Ute had requested a turquoise Zuni bracelet from Tort and, of course, had ended up with a dozen of them that she never wore outside of The Hide. And the night of her visit to the Pfeiffers', even though Mama hadn't offered anything to eat, Dorothee had found a reason to stay long past dinner time. Having exhausted the topic of wild food, she raised herself slowly from her chair and glided out the door and down the stairs. Ute stood at the window and watched the benevolent figure cross the yard. This was a long time ago.

Foolishness, for any of the Pfeiffers, was a state worse than anger.

Mama said that Papa and Dorothee had carried on as though no one had noticed. She had had something of a breakdown, and even that wasn't enough. Somewhere along the line, she took Ute away so that Papa could bring his situation with Dorothee Völker-Stein to an end—which is when Berti got brought into it. Papa and Dorothee had been out walking near the Jesuitengarten with the dog. Felix Stein followed them in his car and only drove at Papa to scare him. He braked but Berti got the force of a decelerating Mercedes. Felix Stein had the most expensive car in all of the Pfalz and he had just used it to run over a spaniel.

Felix offered the use of his helicopter to get Berti to the vet. They went in Papa's car instead. Berti survived the journey but had to be put down anyway. This had been just before Ute and her mother got back from Baden-Baden. But the story was over, Mama didn't have the strength to continue. Like the war brought on by the vanity of Lothar Pfeiffer and friends, this was another bewildering catastrophe caused by man's wish to damage something that has nothing to do with him in the first place.

Ute had always assumed that her mother would be the one to have an affair. She always hoped Mama would run away with one of the firemen whose station backed onto the Pfeiffers' yard. One of them, Josef, had round cheeks and round glasses and Ute liked the way he removed his helmet and clicked his heels together whenever they passed the entrance to the fire station. And Papa probably had felt he was entitled to an affair or two. Ute had always seen them as her entitlement, too. Since nothing anyone would ever do compared to hoarding eyeballs, being related to Lothar Pfeiffer let you off the hook. You could do whatever you wanted.

—How long did this go on?

—Did it stop after Berti you mean? I don't think it ever did. But I have never counted it in years. Twenty, thirty, forty. More.

—All my life then.

Mama hadn't needed to share any of this but she must have wanted to. Hence the shirt, hence the loafers, hence the plan to eat on Felix Stein's boat. Having offloaded all of this, it was suggested that Ute wear something a bit smarter and more colourful than normal for lunch on the Sankt Hedwig. After the morning Ute had had it felt like a perfectly natural request.

With that, Mama, who liked to eat something sweet after smoking, announced her intention to buy Papa some teacakes as a treat for breakfast

There didn't seem to be anyone on board the Sankt Hedwig this morning. She found herself drawn along the gangway to the boat—certainly a craft from another world and another time, the interior designer's idea of a nineteenth-century aristocrat's dining room, overdone in the way of so many of the hotels she had stayed in with Tort. The space was dominated by two oval tables better suited to a grand dining hall. The tables were laid with glasses as shiny as lasers. There was a Biedermeier chandelier with five candles just like the one at home—and a small brass bell which she rang, expecting attention.

She knelt down, out of view of anyone passing along the dock, and examined the morning's delivery. The water was a brand she had looked for but never found in Ireland. She was tempted to help herself to a bottle of the wine, but Mama would have thought that strange and, apart from his daily basin of schnapps, Papa was not one for alcohol anymore. Ute wanted to take one of the bottles and sit on the riverside in the sun and drink it alone, waving at the police boats and the barge men. It wasn't an uncommon sight in summer, someone drinking by the river.

There were some thoughts she wouldn't have minded drinking away. Instead of it being Papa, it was as though

Ute had been the one caught cheating—which had never actually happened, not officially.

Ute had had lovers of her own, but not that many. At first, she had feared everything to do with other men until she discovered that such a feeling was surely fear borne from excitement. Neal, from Andrew Edmunds, was always there and always happy to make himself scarce, and the combination of the two was hard to resist. It was at first just a glass of Riesling after work. He was the first to say that delving into each other's arrangements outside work—getting their colleagues involved, gradually amassing intimacies and expectations—just wasn't going to happen.

When she had first moved into Tort's place on Great Marlborough Street, it was Ute's habit to eat alone after she got in late from work. It was her habit to have mint tea after dinner, which she drank humming along to Mahler, even though there was something unnerving about beautiful music played at such low volume. It was also her habit to leave the house around midnight to walk to a shabby Irish bar just off Dean Street and her habit to meet Neal there and for him to organise the room in which they had sex and to avoid confrontation with Tort in the morning with talk of Mahler.

She still wondered how it all came about. The logistics, the coming and going, and the lying. It wasn't the sex that turned her on, it was the lying. By which she meant, she was a worse person for all of this.

Then Neal went back on his word. He tried to wedge himself into her daily life with well-conceived plans for excursions and even more generous invitations to lunch on their days off—whose schedule he could synchronise—and occasionally dinner. He gathered quickly enough, which was to his credit, that nothing substantial was developing between them, and Ute made sure to stress that nothing would. Their problem, if they had one, was actually much the same as what happened to Tort and her from time to time. She went through long phases of being not that interested in other people and, when she was, she made things difficult for herself by being interested in the wrong ones.

She did not get around to telling Tort that she had been seeing Neal—who continued to make himself very available to her, it was that straightforward—or that she kept on seeing him. Ute moved from working at Andrew Edmunds to a better-paid job at the Criterion on Piccadilly and, even then, she kept on seeing Neal, all the while wondering when and how Tort would find out.

Her bad conscience meant she brought him lamb shanks and ratatouille from the restaurant, not leftovers but full meals that she had to pay for. He usually ate everything—dutifully, no matter the hour—even though he would have had dinner already. One night he left a note to say that he was a little tired and if she would be so kind as to leave the food in the fridge he would have it for breakfast. It was the careful and lawyerly tone he'd used in the note that made her realise that not only did he know what she was up to with Neal, but he was getting fed up with it. Or it could have been that, at last, she was fed up with Neal? The call to say that it was over between them took no longer than it would have done to book a table at the restaurant.

She began then to spend all her free time with Tort, which was more an admission of guilt than anything else. The lead-up to bedtime was the most difficult, an hour she would fill with a long bath and more underpowered Mahler. This was all so long ago she may as well have been making it up. After Neal, she vowed to never again feel so reckless and from then on she was unable to submit to negative thoughts or extravagantly positive ones. All these years later, she was still incapable of extreme reactions. She was capable only of caution.

Ute did one more check to make sure nobody was around. She used her fingernail to pierce the tape before opening the box and removing the first layer of cardboard. The wine was called Völker Ruppertsberg Sekt. Underneath that, in an ugly cursive, was written Cuvée Dorothee alongside a tacky illustration: a woman—not any Dorothee Ute had ever met—draped in a sheet that couldn't cope with her protruding nipples. The top layer contained three bulbous bottles with champagne corks. She removed the foil—heavy, denoting expense—and the wire closure before removing the cork with a firm, choking motion she had seen Tort do on so many festive mornings. The next cork was stiff, which could have been due to the heat. She managed to open it, then another, and then there were three foaming bottles of Sekt lined up at her feet.

The Völker-Steins owned much of the land between there and Luxembourg—so they could have done without a few bottles of their own wine.

Tort placed teaspoons in unfinished bottles of champagne, and she saw him here, weeping over the spilt wine and passing comment on the glasses—stemware, he called it—and on the illustrated Dorothee, who would have been right up his straße.

What would Seanie have made of all of this? She

wouldn't have wished her family story on anyone, but she did wish he was near at hand now. Rambling up Neckarwiese, in something of a daze, as if he'd been canoeing, or taking out the bins, in the wrong clothes for July, what a picture—to appraise the situation before arming them both with the best words: cheerful or soul-enhancing or dopey, it wouldn't matter what he had to say.

Seanie didn't know much about her, this was one of the best things about him. He was blessedly ignorant of all that Tort had worked so hard to assimilate, Lothar Pfeiffer and all that. But the more she thought about it—and this may have been her first time—the more difficult it was to truly align Seanie with Tort and then her family. They separated themselves, all by themselves. She wanted to be with Seanie because her chest told her she did. Falling in love was supposed to be as straightforward as choosing an outfit, but she knew better than anyone—years after deciding to leave Tort but doing nothing about it—that choices were meaningless unless they were acted upon.

The contents of bottle number three sluiced onto the laid deck and overboard through the rail. The deck was scattered with the wire closures, which she pocketed in case of consumption by the ducks and geese that gathered around here. She discarded the corks so that they might bob around in the water and be seen later, hopefully around lunchtime.

She replaced the foil on the bottles and hid them in the box underneath the ones she hadn't touched. She was tempted to shake those up, too, but she was hoping to order some Cuvée Dorothee at lunch later and she didn't want anyone to go without.

He'd be the better for a rinse. To Les Insouciantes, where most certainly Dagmar had gone hell for leather at the Underberg and the Goldschlager. She stank of turps and in place of talking could only waft her hands in the air.

She drew a finger across her throat when he asked if he could take a wash downstairs.

Seanie could only assume an elk had been in to use the bathroom before him. There was a spindrift of hot water and some old pink soap for lathering. The chlorine notes took him all the way back to Donnellan's of Cloonfad. As was his wont, he sang to himself an old ballad with many verses then a whistle of the *Dam Busters'* theme to mark his favourite time of day.

Clean as you like, a quick run through Gundel's for a cake box dainty under the arm. Something with nougat for Christa and playing it safe with currant buns for Ute and the dad. Then to the sombre yard and mossy stones of Bauamtsgaße where many's the morning he'd spent talking to the hen, back when they were on speaking terms.

Not much to be seen at his old windows (he'd have to drop in for his bags), and there, as if arranged, was Ute on the steps waiting. There was no interest in any cakes and niceties. They had cageyness bred into them, this lot.

—There's nougat here. I got it for your mother but you can have it.

—I have everything I need. Mama already bought some cakes.

She wanted to get straight onto the arrangements. Straight to the garage with them to look at the car. More holy importance and exaltation in the admin.

Anything to do with the Pfeiffers had a Gothic bent to it from Julius's old glass, and our hero was not at all immune to the ecclesiastical glint. There, in the yellow light from an old bulb, he was asked for his driving licence, after which he was presented with a plan: Ute and her mother were going out for lunch. And Julius liked to be taken to the vineyard.

No point in troubling her with where he'd spent the night. But Seanie thought he might strap Julius into the Beetle for a spin up the mountain.

—I can open the windows in the car, get a bit of air about him.

—Do you know Wilhelmsfeld? she said.

—By name.

—There's a youth hostel, I'm not sure if anyone uses it, but the building used to belong to his family. He might like to see it. Could you?

—I could.

She shook her head at another offer of the nougat. And that was twice he'd asked her.

—You'll notice I didn't go to Ireland, he said.

—I have packed a bag, she said. With some lunch for him, some bread and sausage. There is just a little schnapps for him. None for you.

She went to get her dad. It was no easy job at all to get Julius strapped into the car, but Seanie knew to act all butlery in these situations. Click the heels, jawohl.

—Julius, he said. What do you say we knock the top off a few nettles?

Up they went through villages from some other century. Up and up past a picturesque amount of cows, the highland cattle quite at home in this terrain. The misty layers of spruce, and a knife of clear sky before it was lost behind more fairy-tale trees.

The higher the climb the humbler the houses. You could only imagine a great sighing at windows. Sunken woodpiles, army nets, wind chimes the colour of the flag. Passing some painted granite rocks, Julius almost clobbered into the windscreen, giving instructions to back up the Beetle.

What kind of place was this at all? The answer was a back road on a mountain attached to another mountain. They rumbled into the yard and up to an old house, its structure in crisis, bare concrete vying with putrid wood. The insolence of the wild grass and no little panache in the painting of the sign: Jungendherberge.

Seanie had never been one for youth hostels—too many hippies—but behold another woodpile, meticulously stacked, and, speaking of happier times, a listing bouncy castle. There were bonfires in the works, a tree carved into half a bear, and a beast of a rose bush with a chained goat nibbling at the thorns. It had to be some kind of fairy-tale place to hold Julius in such rapture.

They got out of the car. Seanie's thoughts were drowned out by the fierce work of a woodpecker. As soon as he went in behind the woodpile for a crafty leak, Julius decided on taking himself off for a walk. Seanie found him staring down into an old quarry.

The first set of steps were descended nimbly enough, but the long slope that followed was more of a challenge. Those old stones were lying in wait to kill someone.

Julius scorned the link of an arm.

Try and he'd burst you, the fists on him like bags of coal.

He made a grab at the wall, his arms raised and rolled in a move from swimming-pool callisthenics. Moving warily and sideways, one step at a time, feet splayed and knees raising slowly. There was reason to believe the old man was being operated from above by strings.

There was a near-stumble but on life went. A little high-kick then, by way of celebration. Now he was just standing there, agog in his own way, head cocked as though listening to music (a little 'Edelweiss'). Sucking his finger, sucking his thumb—the poor man in the mists.

Then he began to mosey. The yearning as he stared into the quarry.

Seanie began to pat his thigh, as though cajoling an old Labrador. Out of Julius came a tuneless sound, more of a sean-nós than a croon. A bow of the head and another lament to notify the Lord.

Seanie pulled him back from the edge. He was lip-smacking and staring, expressing nothing and feeling nothing.

—Ah jaysus, Julius. Julius!

He'd bitten his own tongue. Bloodied mouth and chin, the tongue a crimson slug.

And it came down upon them like a summer storm: Julius's life, and here it was over. You could only wonder at the memories, their awful noise. In Julius's folk tale, there'd be fairies in the woodpile, snakes in the woodpile—a frightened boy who wouldn't look under the bed. The boy sees under the bed. The boy climbs out of the window and runs away.

Like fuck down the mountain. In the car, the first-aid kit was unpromising, the cotton wool was unpromising, the entire scenario was unpromising. Julius's mouth was clamped shut, Seanie had his hands in there. Raising the question, what were they going to do now? He increased the speed through more hunkered villages, the laws of civilisation re-imposing themselves.

Julius gave a soft sigh then, the manner of which implied a state of ecstasy and great comfort. Cheeks shining, a sweet peace about him, and all the folk tales were long gone to the mountain.

The old man's crotch had darkened. The indignity of old age with infanthood's ornaments.

—That better? Seanie said with a sigh of his own.

For there was a sudden slice of water, and the great gentleness of Heidelberg becoming visible. The spires and the university soundless and busy. The old bridge packed as an airport, the river's filigree, and the paddleboats gathering in expectation of another afternoon on the water.

Sankt Hedwig

Mama had seen cut tongues before and not even childbirth was more painful. Papa got stripped and changed where he stood, holding onto the back of a chair while cotton wool was pushed into his mouth. Mama was doing her job now, her fury directed inwards, as though she and not Seanie were responsible for Papa's injury.

Mama called Dr Reuter and it was not until she eliminated the quiver from her voice that they were told go immediately to the surgery. Papa, reluctant to be parted from Seanie once more, uttered his first words in a couple of days—an aside about the poor driving.

Ute had relinquished all control of the day the moment she'd seen Mama occupying her patch of morning sun at the kitchen table. Now, seemingly by her design, she and Seanie were alone.

—I assume this is the last time I'll be looking after your father. The state of him.

—They'll fix him up.

—There's a possibility that I took my eye off the ball.

—Please, I think you are experiencing guilt for something you haven't done.

—That would be called shame, I can do ashamed for you all day. But you've enough on your plate with having to be my psychiatrist.

—I wouldn't know how much to charge.

—I've been coming and going from the idea that I should say sorry for the going away.

—You said you were going away and you went away. That is one more thing that does not come under the heading of sorry.

—You have it sussed, so. I'd a small notion that I'd upset you.

—Never, she said. Not you. And it's such a pity that Mama has left me with no lunch companion.

Ute was to be congratulated on the smooth delivery of such a line. Sometime that morning, perhaps around the time of her escapade on the Sankt Hedwig, she must have decided to make the best of things.

The Neckar was behaving as if it were lost and as if it were hurt, the brown water dragging itself hesitantly past the Sankt Hedwig. Ute was returning to the scene of the crime, her secret divulging itself in the sight of the Sekt corks floating in the water. The young waiter standing on deck watched them make their way along the quayside. He snuffed his cigarette as though he couldn't stand to part with it.

—On you go, Seanie said, standing aside. He was considering the boat deeply.

The young waiter was the kind of clean-cut and accordingly vain officer type that Ute had once convinced herself she found attractive, and he was affronted that they were seeking lunch at a minute past two. Perhaps he wanted retribution for his gulped cigarette. In the time it took for Ute to make her way along the gangway, her nerve deserted her to join the corks in the water.

The dining room was empty and, not counting whomever was in the kitchen below deck, there were four uniformed staff on duty. Ute and Seanie were left alone while the waiter went to consult with an older man who was sitting at one of the empty tables. Ute hadn't laid eyes on Felix Stein in years. He and the young waiter had the same severe hairstyle, which had been popular in the nineteen-forties and eighties as well as now, and were wearing the same defeated expression. He certainly looked like a billionaire called Felix Stein was supposed to look like. His arms were sinewy and hairless and the colour of brass, and couldn't have been the arms of an eighty-year-old.

His age seemed to have nothing to do with the vanquished way he was examining the bubbles in his glass, counting them one by one.

Seanie was rotating his head to get a look at the room.

—I get fidgety in nice places, he whispered.

—How do we know how nice it is until they let us sit down?

—Chandeliers on a boat say nice to me.

The young waiter finished his conversation with Felix Stein and walked ahead to offer Ute the run of the room. She sat on a banquette alongside Seanie so that she could keep an eye on all the goings-on. It helped to be partially blinded by the sun—she could gaze at the golden room and imagine her father and Dorothee Völker-Stein having lunch together; as reckless a daydream as she would permit herself at that moment.

Liverwurst, dumplings, saumagen, fleischkäse. The lightest option, in thirty-degree heat, appeared to be goose fat on rye bread. The Völker-Steins were sure to have a potager at home in Forst, and a gardener—or maybe Dorothee took care of all that. Some vegetables could have made their way to the Sankt Hedwig occasionally. She was damn sure that Felix Stein didn't eat any of the food on this menu. If only Ute had brought some of the salad leaves she had seen growing wild this morning. They would have been at their sappy best picked at that time of the day. She could have run home now and made a point of presenting them as a gift in her mother's wicker basket.

—No schnitzels? Seanie said. He was humming to himself, and moving his knees like a drummer's.

—Schnitzel, as you know, is an Austrian speciality, she replied helpfully. Wiener.

—Vienna. Noted. I like an egg on my schnitzel.

Some people became children in restaurants. And she didn't mean behaving poorly, they revealed themselves. As someone who had written about them professionally, albeit at a low level, she was well aware how being in a restaurant, how being out, could alter perception and raise expectations. She might have been falling for him, and might have done so already, and his awkwardness around menus and cutlery and glassware should have reminded her not to, but it didn't.

The cooking smells pervading the dining room took her back to the longing of Sunday afternoons. Chores and homework and shoe polish. One afternoon, after they had been to the vineyard, Ute was acting busy while her father polished glass at the old table in the kitchen. Her parents were discussing a significant purchase Papa wanted to make. He was telling Ute's mother not to worry about the expense, that he was expecting a good year at the glass-maker's and he wanted to celebrate it with something significant for the house—a new table. Mama would often rub beeswax into the warp of their existing table and every night would devoutly adjust the beer mats under the legs at one side. Run a pfennig along the top and as often as not it would roll off, sometimes to be forgotten. Ute was allowed to save the stray pennies. In the morning Papa would exasperatedly remove the beer mats and bemoan their sloping floors and provincial taste. He displayed a sage leaf to illustrate the elliptical oblong's origin in nature. When the new table arrived, so that she could properly absorb the curve, which was more beautiful than any leaf or anything she had ever seen in nature, Ute sat for hours on the floor, eye level with the tabletop. It occurred to her now that her father had based this significant purchase—the new table about which Dorothee Völker-Stein had been so complimentary—on the furniture at the Sankt Hedwig.

The young waiter returned, listlessly but with free soup in a cup. Ute supposed it was approaching the season for corn chowder. He put it just out of their reach.

—No customers, Seanie said. Seventy members of staff. And they're still giving out free stuff. I love this country. I really hope you win the World Cup.

Seanie was always serious and yet not serious. Ute saw in this and the way he had been with Papa an old-fashionedness that she found so charming. That word again. Everything Seanie said was important and unimportant.

He toasted her with an empty wine glass. Why on earth his smile caught her by surprise she had no idea. It was not on the menu but she decided then she would ask them to make Wiener schnitzel. Why not? She raised her arm and the waiter approached so momentously slowly that he was surely being sarcastic. He was making it easy for her to pick him off. But, Ute's tone was brisker than she intended when she said they would like something special to eat.

The waiter paid another visit to the top table, where he said something that made Felix Stein rise nimbly from his seat and make his way towards them carrying the bottle of Cuvée Dorothee. Ute was acknowledged courteously but sceptically. Evidently Felix Stein recognised her but couldn't place her, and this suited her down to the ground. The EXIT sign was framed just over his head as he examined their glasses and found a napkin with which to polish them. He poured half-glasses of Sekt and announced that they were the first people to taste the new vintage, and to mark the occasion he would have the cook make whatever they would like to eat.

—Pork or veal? he said.

—Veal, Seanie said.

—Of course, Ute said, and thanked Felix Stein's back as he went off to instruct the cook.

The richest man in the Pfalz was seeing to their lunch and she had no idea why. She supposed it was for his own amusement. He was probably one of those bosses who made a point of never asking his staff to do anything he wouldn't do himself. Those kinds of people were a terror to work for.

Seanie sipped the wine and said something about champagne and the compulsion in a certain class of German to imitate the French.

—You could do something with that vineyard.

—It's an acre.

—It's an acre of fucking paradise is what it is.

—There's a man that goes there sometimes, a family friend. Have you seen him?

—Horse of a man? I've seen him, he's seen me. I'd nearly say there was a bang of the pharaoh off him, patron saint.

—He's a very gentle man.

—He's the cut of someone who'd hear a good confession.

—Have you ever spoken to him?

—I'd be scared to.

—You'd feel better afterwards.

—I'll chance it next time I see him. I'll give him a few quid for the church roof.

—But you're right, Ute said. The place needs looking after.

Every June Papa would organise a picnic in the vineyard to celebrate the bottling of the previous year's wine. He resisted the word 'barbecue'. It was a picnic in the dearly beloved vineyard. He would spend days ferrying supplies up to the Philosophers' Walk in his van. Trestle tables were covered in old wallpaper. Benches were positioned so that everyone had a view of the schloß or the river. The menu resembled what was on offer at the Sankt Hedwig today—this was just the food everyone ate thirty years ago. Papa cooked everything on a wood fire, taking more care than was necessary with the cooking of the asparagus even though it was the end of the season and they would be as sturdy as rolling pins. Ute liked sausages, the spicy feuerwurst which Papa said killed the taste of the wine she wasn't old enough to drink and didn't like. Mustard was banned for the same reason. You could count on Papa to take great care with the glasses—the green-stemmed Römers—but disregard basic things like enough cutlery to go around, which implied disapproval of anyone who was more interested in the food than the wine. Papa classified his friends by their attitude to his wines, preferring those who lingered obligingly over a single glass of Promise Me the Mountain. There wasn't that much to go around anyway, there was only an acre of vines.

People didn't mingle. They found a bench and stuck to it. Everyone would be gone by ten. She didn't remember the Völker-Steins ever being there.

There was from downstairs a sound resembling an explosion—the meat entering hot oil. Hardly moments later, Felix Stein appeared before them in an apron bearing his name. He was carrying a platter bearing six schnitzels the size of pillowcases. The garnish of parsley was the perkiest Ute had ever seen.

Felix Stein took a step back and measured her up once more before hauling himself back to his table, where he was joined by the young waiter and another one—a tall, slender girl with bulky bracelets. Ute would not have been surprised to hear that they were connected to Dorothee in some way.

Seanie's eyes widened like there was something he wanted to say to the food.

—I should warn you I eat fast.

—You're hungry, she said.

—So fast that I get out of breath.

—If I'd known that I wouldn't have asked you on a date.

Seanie looked suddenly vulnerable among all the slippery light—reflections from the water, the glasses, the windows, the wine glasses. He guided some food towards his plate then changed his mind before filling hers.

—If I'd known we were going to be going on one of those, he said.

As things were, this was exactly like a first date.

On the riverbank opposite, Ute could see people commendably and enviably undone by exercise, lunchtime revellers undone by insects and cheap alcohol, which was inadvisable in the heat but all their own business. On the quay beside the Sankt Hedwig there was a Japanese girl undone by the effort of posing for multiple photographs and, perhaps, the thought of past or future sex. It was the most beautiful thing Ute had seen all summer, and it didn't at all remind her of Seanie.

That morning she had been considering the idea of a clean river—not the murky water she saw now—pouring through her at the point of climax. More and more she was coming to think of her insides as a slow-moving river in summer.

One of the new cruisers passed alongside the Sankt Hedwig. Ute heard the recorded commentary and turned to find herself under review by several cruise-takers, including one with a pair of binoculars. It was not a particularly unpleasant prospect—being inspected as though you were a rare penguin—and she was delighted to be, from their point of view, the mysterious lady diner on the strange old boat.

—What happened with you and your girlfriend? Ute said. Or is it prying to ask about your romantic status?

—Quaint phrase. Romantic. I'm single for the first time in years.

—Do you mind that? Ute said.

—It wasn't my choice, if that's what you're asking. Then again, we might have been a bit hasty in the first place. I got on the first bus that was leaving the station, so to speak. And some bus she was. She did have her tender side, we did have our tender moments, but they were few and far between.

—That's not very nice.

—I'm being funny about it, but I don't feel very funny.

—What did you do?

—I got angry then I cried.

—I don't like the idea of anyone crying.

—I'll never do that again, if I can help it.

—And then you decided to stay. The magnetic forces of the Neckar drew you back?

—I get assaulted by the notion that I might even like it. The softness, aforementioned. But going to a place like Germany and having a nice time for yourself, there even being sunshine, it gives you very contrary thoughts.

—It's the same sun as everywhere else. We're an hour from a France. Two hours from Italy.

—I know where we *are*, we're light years from fucking anywhere. You have to want to be here to come here. It could be the river, it goes too slow, it's in a daze, it's trying to hypnotise you and have its way.

—Have you swum in it?

—And I've swallowed half of it, it's more diesel than water.

—You're not supposed to swim. There are rules, I don't know what they are, but there are some.

—Say no more, Seanie said. I don't want to give anyone the wrong impression, but I might have come back to see someone in particular.

He was highly absorbed in his second piece of veal. She studied his lips, plump and greasy and pursed in concentration on the muslin-covered lemon. This morning she had woken up wanting to be with him—to be with him, then see him off the premises—and had gone as far as picturing them together. Her initial attraction to him, which fell under the loose heading of lust, was not the same attraction she had now, observing him already moving onto his third schnitzel.

—Your father eats like a horse, he said.

—He enjoyed his lunch? It was only sausage and bread.

—Indeed and he did enjoy his lunch. Until he took lumps out of himself.

—I'll make him something else tomorrow. Soup is easier on the tongue.

—I think being up there at the youth hostel took its own toll.

—Did he tell you about my grandfather?

—I wouldn't exactly say we are close confidants.

—You're as close as he has to one.

She was simply glad to hear that Papa had gone somewhere other than the vineyard for once. But she could feel her face lighting up. She ripped the muslin away from the lemon and squeezed juice on her empty plate.

—My grandfather was a professor of ophthalmology. His specialised subject was people with eyes of a different colour, as a sign of weakness. Whenever he found a prisoner with different-coloured eyes, he would have them cleared away so he could study the eyes. He had a collection like sweets in a jar.

Seanie adjusted his position on the banquette so that he was looking right at her. She couldn't tell what was in his mouth, but he did something with his throat that may or may not have been a gulp. It was as if he didn't understand what Lothar Pfeiffer had really done, or she hadn't successfully made her point, or he was being courteous.

He looked directly at her to say, —I'm sure you've dealt with it, in your own way.

—It's not something you can deal with. You just think there's something wrong with you when there isn't.

She had had to lower her voice so she wouldn't be heard by the Völker-Steins, for whom the new wine and this empty boat seemed to be a very big deal. Dorothee, wherever she was, would have had fun here today. The wine that bore her name and her nipples wasn't too bad at all.

—I'm sorry if I make it all sound so matter of fact. It's not a pretty story for a nice lunch. We could talk about something else. What about the wine?

Ute tried to get a glimpse of the bobbing corks. At their table, the gathered Völker-Steins were beginning on another bottle of Sekt. Now she surprised herself by not being finished with the subject of Lothar Pfeiffer, and that she was crying. The story was not new to her, and she didn't want Seanie to think that she needed comforting. That was the rule with sharing anything strange or sad. It was always worse for the other person, even when the bearer was ashamed of the news they were delivering.

Seanie leaned in, his face astream with something like helpfulness. As if she were about to feed them to her father, Ute started slicing up the remaining schnitzels. She smiled at the way her morning had ended, in bobbing corks and disarray and a sort of triumph.

—I don't think I've ever talked so much about myself in my life, she said.

The fucking look she threw at him when he said that the only thing to do was jump into the river.

The suit needed an airing, he said, it was sending out animal notes. He wasn't long getting out of it, with the breeze making soft circuits of his privates and his breath shortening with wistfulness. Ute was stripping down to the mightiness of herself.

They unlatched the gate at the stern of the boat, the gleam in Ute's eye, and the one in Seanie's.

—Sure you're sure about this?

—Don't ask that now, she said.

The world of schnitzels and off the side of a boat with them. Cheers rising from folk onshore.

The river had had its way, finally. The Neckar was bog-warm, and his blood also was at temperature. There was a bit of sweet wind rising and the brazen light was dancing, the sun flashing on the water and in their eyes. Ute was a little while getting used to it but sure as anything they were floating easy now. It was just like having a rest or a nice bath, and he was alone with her and she was alone with him just like he'd dreamed they might, and there wasn't much to it, with the day's kindly way of looking on them, and if they wanted to they could have stayed like this all afternoon.

He hauled her onto the riverbank. She came up out of the water glistening. You could, he thought, capsize your own boat through the simple act of awe.

He turned his eyes to the sky and was expecting in that very moment for her to have disappeared. For doubt was his master, he was forever sighing it out of himself.

He'd had a girlfriend, our hero had had a girlfriend, he'd had a girlfriend and—he sighed more doubt.

Slowly the facts of the matter were grasped. In the suggestive heat of an afternoon, there was solace to be found in the place still.

On the way up from the river, for fear she might have said she was going home, Seanie fell into the story about his dad.

—I got into a spot of bother a few years ago. Something bad happened without me doing much to cause it. If I'd known I could kill people just by looking crooked at them I'd do it more often. It's like being given the credit for scoring a goal when the ball didn't touch your foot. No, it's the opposite of that. Lookit, I didn't kill anyone, but there was a picture in the local paper of my dad at the finish line of the half-marathon and someone sent it to the house. You could die fiddling crusts out of the toaster.

He could have said anything he wanted but the sense of duty in sticking to the true line of the tale: the pubs, the police, the aftermath, each scene taking on new light and less weight with another go-around in the telling. He could've done with a different ending, but if you went that way you'd spend half your life picking at threads.

He broke off by saying it had been a long old bank holiday weekend, but the truth of it was Seanie and his dad had been having a nice time for themselves.

Afterwards, outside Les Insouciantes, he was afraid to look at her. He was drinking slowly, as if out of courtesy for the occasion. Only when Ute slipped her feet out of her sandals and rested them on his did he feel the strain of expectations returning to his life.

—The cobbles are still warm, she said.

—Very obliging of them.

—Take off your shoes?

There and then he'd've accepted dropping dead.

—The pong would clear the square, he said.

—Can I ask a question? she said.

—Of course.

—What if you don't like it?

—I'll not answer it.

—Why the suit?

—It's part of me. You can ask another one if you like.

—You've been wearing it for a few days now.

—I'm still breaking it in. What do you make of it?

—It's thought-provoking.

—Same as that. The weave is very forgiving, and the weight. You could go through a hedge in it.

—And sleep in one?

—If need be, and no one need know.

This being her way, Ute fell quiet now and again. Feeling it an intrusion to talk, he took care to hold the silence. But before long he was gibbering as if being paid by the word.

The topic was home, and the job of work it was to get yourself out of the way of the machinery of Irish life, machinery that ran on savagery and spite. The place was run by clowns and bastards, but, if the ways of the world could be overwhelming, Cloonfad had made its own arrangements. The maelstrom was avoided through the past times of shite talk and desperation, to which Donnellan father and son had the ready access of publicans.

Then it came to dancing. The Donnellan men could jive, they could twist, and they could waltz with the best of them. The thought crossed Seanie's mind that this was in some way connected to their nerves.

Show Noel Donnellan a yard of lino and the Boylans slip-ons would be blurring. There'd be insects in his socks, dancing with one and sizing up the next. The end of the night would be put to him like a bereavement, he'd have to be led away by the elbow.

—I dare say you can dance, Seanie said.

—Well trained, she said.

They fell into the idea of a drink on Untere Straße. The one they had called for another, and so they were strapped in for the night. She had the bright idea then to go to her dad's old local.

In Susanna's they served nothing but room-temperature Müller-Thurgau. Legend had it that if you drank enough you hallucinated in the old-fashioned way: theremins and vibrating flagstones. It was where the hurt and weary of the town congregated. The staff from the prison, women and men who had taken all those mad little pills in the sixties. If you were too hurt or weary to get home for dinner, and she liked you, Susanna would make you a brötchen with honey and butter. Seanie had never had one.

Ute Pfeiffer's entrance was something of an event. Looking on were the souls who'd dedicated their lives to drinking small tumblers of weak white wine, answerable to no one but Susanna.

Seanie knew them all by name. Maxime was four foot tall and smoked cheroots. The tone of varnish to her, and, indeed, the dimensions of a very small chair. Rumour had it that she survived on wine and beef tea, and in the sixties had carried a pistol with which she shot two separate lovers in the head. People left her be. Next to her, a man called Magnus was brushing ash from a shiny football top that was too small on him. Magnus was in residence with his pet wolf, the pair of them twenty-six glasses and two honey-and-butter brötchen into another day of public rumination. No one there to talk them out of their twenty-seventh.

Magnus was tapping his feet and choking back sick. There was only so much Müller-Thurgau a man could drink without it eating him from the inside. But the smoky room was lit like heaven, and, on hearing 'I Got You Babe', Seanie felt he had promised Ute a waltz.

Touched her sleeve and said, —Shall we?

—This isn't a waltz, she said.

—We'll manage.

They settled into it easily enough. It all coming back to him, the diagram in his head, the one-two-three, the steps coming to him more as suggestions than memories.

What he lacked in co-ordination he made up with good intent, but the moves he was making were those of a hesitant, sad man, and Seanie would not have argued with this observation. If he blundered once or twice it was also on account of the lamplight reflecting on Ute's forehead and cheeks, the red and cream and gold. Soon he stopped bothering to hide the fact of his stare. Not only was he able to look right at her, there was relief in her practice of giving nothing away. She could've outstared a seagull. Most certainly he was being held in her arms, there was kindness in the way she was following him, and soon they were making better shapes, cutting nicely through the smoke. Foot to foot they went. With every box step and every glance from their own feet to each other's, it struck him that the onlookers took them to be lovers. The dance was an act of love, yes. They both made a certain amount of missteps but one of hers was down to a sleeping wolf being in the way. Politely Seanie said to Magnus, honest to God would you fucking move the animal.

On they moved with the moments taking on the kind of stillness he felt to be intimacy. What faced him was simple and straightforward: already they had found themselves on intimate terms.

Dancing was like life but easier.

But Seanie was soon in the way of himself, he was dancing on sand. One thing Dad had always told him was to imagine a parachute, and you were pulling one after you. But there was the sound of breathing (it was his own and it unnerved him) and he couldn't picture the parachute, he was sure he could hear it dragging on the ground. Even Dad was saying, it's like you don't know the first thing about dancing, get those breaths in order, in through the nose out through the mouth, go again, remember your steps (he was truly giving out advice on steps), and if you're not going to believe in yourself you should pack it up, pull into the hard shoulder.

Ute then got him out of it with a movement so fluid that it could never have been prepared for. There was no need for this one to be shown a puzzle before solving it. She leaned as she went so that she seemed to be dancing downhill, or away from him. Was she adjusting to his weaker side? How did she know it was his weak side? Her body was receiving messages.

A sniff through one nostril denoted consent for the dancers to join Maxime's table, them being received as if under great sufferance. But there was surprisingly little menace in the invitation. Up close there was a certain aroma of sheep. And was she of ages with Julius? This was the point, mein schatz, this was the point.

Seanie wasn't catching everything, but the thing of it was that she knew Ute Pfeiffer, for she knew Julius Pfeiffer, and the tone hoarse but sweet as they heard how Maxime had loved him as she had loved no one else. The hands on her no bigger than the hen's feet, them shaking, and the cheroot burning away madly as it came to her that the birth of this man was one of the Lord's great gifts to the world. She would steal up the hill to spy on him, and the quiet work he did in the vines. She'd steal a leaf or two for herself. Do you know how long it takes for a leaf to rot? Two years she got out of it, one leaf.

Did she ever tell Julius? She did not, not a word. It cut the heart out of her but still she kept an eye, for no one else in the place had Julius Pfeiffer's way with glass. His way with a rotary tool would have put the best dentist to shame.

This carried on sweetly through the years. Her little mouse, her little bear. But the world encroached, and people too, and slowly Maxime fell into the ways she was in now.

They sat tired and easy with one another, like they'd been all day at the hay. They'd had their fill of drink, they'd waltzed, they'd held hands, he'd told her more of his plans, nimbly avoiding any talk of where he was living.

In the morning he'd be asking Dagmar if he could take another wash in Les Insouciantes, and this was not the kind of information you just offered up to people.

The fact that Ute might think less of him had our hero very agitated. But the past was fading all around them, their burden cast into the water at the Sankt Hedwig, a bit more of it on the floor in Susanna's.

Ute asked him to walk her home and, after a passing mention of flinging themselves back into the Neckar, Bauamtsgaße came all too soon. The day's mugginess was falling away to something lighter, he was tempted to use the word 'ethereal'. Ute's demeanour hadn't changed, but he had to believe that she had had a nice time for herself. He wasn't about to ask if he could come in. Julius would be dead to the world, but he knew Christa to be a light sleeper. The thought, and the moment, was inclined towards catastrophe.

The next move was unignorably suave, better even than the thought of them going upstairs, and better again than the swimming and the schnapps and the dancing. The impulse presented itself, and his first thought was to refuse it. But the words were moving through him, and he found himself drawn towards a bit of a performance. No point in being shy about it.

—I've something to say, he said.

—I'm all ears.

—A bit of a poem.

She did not seem in any way impressed, and nor was she put out that he was trying to show off. He knew the words off by heart, he was forever reciting them to himself and the wall. The divine weight in lines and half-lines about skin and dew.

He adjusted his stance, having it in mind that it was matadorish, and that the placement of his feet was an aid to the breathing.

—It's not one of mine, he said.

—Probably for the best.

He could feel the river moving under the cobbles, and all of a sudden the ground underfoot was slippery. His lips moved and by divination nothing came. The lines ran in a hurry to his mouth, and went no further than that.

—I don't think it's coming to me, he said.

Now there was the true depth of night, whereupon the internal workings were more wishes than thoughts. He must have seemed that bit gone. The bones of his head were suddenly thick and heavy and there was the strong rumour of a palpitation.

Her palm was against his cheek. —Don't worry, she said. Give me the name of the poem and I can look it up.

Promise Me the Mountain

Ute awoke so early that it hardly counted as morning, the light in her room—lilac, soft and dissolute—providing refuge for all the absurd and immodest thoughts she had been deferring since the night before.

It had been her idea to go to Susanna's. Everyone crouched over glasses of wine that tasted weak and sharp like Papa's. So it had seemed appropriate that she met a woman who'd lived her life in love with Julius Pfeiffer. Ute had gone to the bathroom every so often just so she could observe everything afresh, the smoke drifting across the old lanterns and these new faces. It was unclear how it had come about but at one point, after they had danced and as they were listening to this Maxime woman, she and Seanie had held hands under the table. The night had positioned her anew; she tried to explain this to Seanie and found herself talking incautiously as if to an old friend and—with Tort elsewhere and Markus long gone to the mountain—Ute didn't have any of those anymore. She went on so long that she must have bored him.

All the talk made her consider one thing: Heidelberg was home—not an idea with which she had ever been enthralled—and it wasn't home; for everyone under that tobacco-rich ceiling seemed to have lost as well as won at life. The sleeping wolf, drunk strangers who could have been friends, all of them soaked in certainty and World Cup optimism and too much old-fashioned wine.

Mama wasn't up yet. Ute made tea and occupied the stripe of sunlight in the kitchen. How beautiful to sit with the dawn glowing and the sky-blue sky promising no rain. This she was going to take personally. Irish skies were always so close or there was no sky at all, or the mist wrapped itself around you in the way of a wet bedsheet. The Irish deemed it unfair that it rained constantly, yet give them five minutes of sun and they misbehaved completely, leaving work at three in the afternoon and calling in sick the next day.

The Berti stones in the yard were more overgrown with moss than ever. Ute could always recognise the section that had been replaced by her father because the cobbles were lined up more neatly than anywhere else in the yard, which was warm and damp and smelling of the earth and what was buried in it. The place in ruins gave her an idea that seemed strange at first. The herbs and weeds had been soaking up all the sunlight and giving nothing back.

Ute, too, had been here long enough—it was time to get to work, and this was work best done at dawn.

Without weedkiller there was nothing she could do about the moss on the cobbles themselves. First she ran a hose and soaked the yard so the weeds would come out at the root.

In under an hour she had collected enough dandelions and amaranth, purslane and lamb's quarters to keep them in salad for a week. Although her nerves were jagged, she had felt vaguely delighted all morning; the amusement was coming in sudden shards. Hangovers absolved you of all reason and this one, her first in years, was a pleasant warning. The day and night she'd spent with Seanie was a sign, too, although of what she had yet to determine.

Perhaps she had gone back in time, just a few days. This was a chance to retrieve the optimism she had come home with, and had forgotten, and which no one would have begrudged her.

She found herself dripping wine sweat as she filled the compost with the greens she couldn't identify. Mama was moving around inside. It was six o'clock and Ute would have to explain herself with all her weeding, but they weren't going to go through any more of that. Her parents had lost the knack and the will to maintain things, and Ute should have dealt with the upkeep the moment she got here.

Mama opened the window with a smile that loitered around disapproval. The yard resembled a roughly shaven head. It puzzled Ute to think how much she enjoyed the sight of it.

—Need a hand?

—If you can manage it.

—Of course I can manage it.

Mama took a few a minutes to get changed into her old things then danced down the stairs as if a stint in the garden had been the plan all along. But she did not turn out be an acquiescent co-worker—a matron, after all, who was used to things being done a certain way, and things always being wrong.

There was a single pair of gloves. Mama took them and put them on. Without being in any way systematic, she cleared a little glade for herself. It had become hot and weeding would have been gruelling for anyone, but she hummed as she worked, her feet hip-distance apart and her arms swinging. In yoga they called this the rag doll, and her mother, who had never done a single stretch in her life, was a natural. On their last trip to Maastricht to see André Rieu, Tort had diverted them to Antwerp, where they saw a Van Gogh of a peasant woman picking potatoes, and Ute, timid on her hands and knees, thought of this as she drank her mother in.

Mama wandered around the yard to stretch her back and appraise their efforts so far. There was only a vague interest in saving anything to eat as salad.

—Most of this is edible, Mama.

—Nearly everything is edible if you are hungry enough. And Heidelberg has shops.

Ute attempted to tell her about the day with Seanie, and that she'd been to the Sankt Hedwig after all. But Mama with work to do paid no attention.

—I heard you come in. I thought you were fighting with him.

—We weren't fighting.

Mama held Ute's eye and with an air of impatience said, —I thought you were.

—We weren't.

—That's what I hoped but I didn't know. I can tell you now that fighting is no way to conduct a relationship. Your father and I fought and it did neither of us any good. There is no such thing as passion in an argument. A disagreement is a disagreement.

—We weren't even arguing.

—Someone was raising their voice.

Mama, who could be highly alert to other people's emotions without ever being affected by them, scowled at a bit of moss. Ute wondered about revealing what Seanie had really been doing, but her mother would have rationalised his attempted recital as oafishness.

My vegetable love will grow. Vaster than empires and more slow.

But he hadn't been able to remember the rest of the poem, standing back from her as if the air around them was scorched.

Papa seemed lightly excited by the horticultural goings-on. Mama made an exaggerated treat of some soothing yoghurt for breakfast, sitting beside him on the bench in the yard and stopping just short of making an aeroplane noise to get it into his mouth. At Ute's feet were enough damp and glossy stalks to stuff a mattress. It just so happened that she was beginning on the area where Papa had once buried her dog, and Ute worried that the Berti stones would be easily dislodged. But they stayed put.

Papa was looking not at either of them but at the discarded weeds and their slight, spidery roots. He had for most of his life tended an acre of hillside and, to look at him now, he wasn't too troubled to let someone else do the hard graft for once.

Ute wanted to tell him about herself and Seanie, who would be coming over later to take Papa out for the final. It was nobody's business, but Ute enjoyed the fact that she had slyly engineered the entire situation. In which case it was nothing to be proud of.

And yet.

Papa stood up abruptly and took a few steps forwards as though someone had called him.

—Julius, Mama said sharply.

In the time it took for him to sit back down, Papa's expression had moved from curiosity to puzzlement, and was well on the way to the dismay he was directing at his own waggling foot. He bent double to study his slippers, as he often did.

Mama stood up from the Berti stones, squinted at him then leapt into action. She trotted inside and upstairs and returned with some schnapps and ice. One of the photo albums was tucked under her arm.

—It pains me, she said. But we must give him exactly what he wants.

Papa had lived through and forgotten so much, and these albums, and those long-gone holidays, always brought him back to life. The photos had been glued to the pages long ago but he fluttered his hands as if he were arranging them just so. Mama paid no attention—he looked at them every night—but Ute was fascinated by one of Lothar Pfeiffer looking on with great pride as young Papa and his mother were painting the ceramic of a jug with the words *Praise not the day until evening has come*. The annihilation of old age, and its conundrum, was that it took you all the way back to childhood.

The Pfeiffers had weekended at Wilhelmsfeld as often as Ute's grandfather's work allowed. The house was built halfway up a hill—in a wood out of wood—and, whenever Papa had described it, no one else ever went there. It wasn't a castle or a manor house, this fabled place of Papa's childhood was an oversized wooden chalet with an ordinary view of the Baden Odenwald. You couldn't tell much at all from a black-and-white photo taken seventy-five years ago, but it seemed as though the sun had always shone and that there had been great joy and freedom up there in the hills. To look at Papa now—crouched over the album and sucking ice—he was still there in some way.

Ute and Mama were working close to one another, out of his earshot, and it was safe enough as well as the right time to ask the question that had been bubbling overnight.

—Where is Dorothee these days?

Mama didn't look up from her scraping. —Gone.

—You didn't say that yesterday. It was as if she was about to walk in at any moment. Gone where?

—An artists' retreat in Scotland. On the Isle of Mull. The architecture is stunning, if you like that kind of thing. Felix paid for it all. And, tell me, what is it artists have to retreat from exactly?

Mama rummaged in the pile of green at her feet and found a nice broad dock leaf, which she used to blow her nose. The smell of pulled weeds was medicinal and slightly stirring.

—Did you have a nice time yesterday, then?

—Mama.

—I'd like some of that yoghurt. If he doesn't want it.

Mama gave Papa some schnapps. A line of sweat, a map of Chile, ran down the length of her back.

—I don't mean to be emotional, she said. You have lived away from here for too long. But I am not calm and rational when it comes to that woman. And I don't want to rake anything over. Your father and I never spoke about it anyway. There's no point now.

—I do understand the concept of adultery.

Mama was watching her now. In her eyes was surely a fear that she might have to acknowledge Tort further. And she didn't, except to say, —So you know what it's like.

—Yes.

—But you don't know. You were that man's master, I could see it.

—Hardly.

—I was your father's servant. And he needed to know what that felt like, to be that for someone else.

Papa was there, and had been all along. His ice was melting. He was holding out his bowl for more.

—No more, Julius, Mama said. I just filled the tray.

To Tort's question of why they never had any people over to The Hide, Ute had always replied that they had no one to invite.

Once, almost a lifetime ago, Dorothee contacted her to suggest an afternoon by the sea in Dublin. Felix was in Asia to receive another honorary degree—which he wouldn't look twice at—and, since Dorothee wasn't one for that at all, she took the opportunity to do some travelling of her own. She suggested taking a taxi to Wicklow, but Ute, in the unthinking way she went about things then, drove into town for a sandwich at the Shelbourne.

The visit had come out of the blue, but there was nothing behind it. Or at least Dorothee, loose-limbed as ever and smelling of summer elsewhere, didn't give a reason. Her bones gleamed under her skin. The pinstripes on her high-waisted trousers may have been hand sewn, but Ute thought she looked less exceptional than she ever had in Heidelberg. That might just have been down to the dismal light in Ireland.

Ute once thought she had loved Dorothee. After the night of the wild boar delivery, she kept asking her parents about the Völker-Steins, whether she could visit the vineyards in Forst. The answer was always no.

Later in life, she talked about them so much that Tort ordered a case of the Völker Forster Riesling and gave it his approval, saying that drinking it was like standing in a mountain brook at dawn. It became the aperitif he suggested to anyone who was new to German wine. Ute always had a bottle on her birthday. She much preferred it to the wine Papa used to make on the Philosophers' Walk.

Dorothee had wanted to go somewhere special. The best that Dublin had to offer, she said, even though she wasn't in the mood to sign up for a whole afternoon in a restaurant. This may just have been her life, and Ute's to a certain extent, the fate of the supernaturally wealthy to graze; life an exquisite and unamazing buffet, an indefinite overture to a stiflingly unimaginative evening that, as it bored you, you wished would never end. Like having too many orgasms, it wasn't as if anyone could complain.

When Ute said a sandwich would be more appropriate, Dorothee as they ate became much more introspective than Ute had ever imagined she could be. Nor was the conversation very illuminating. Dorothee was in the process of setting up her artists' colony. Her visit to Ireland wasn't exactly a research trip, but they had to find something to talk about. Ute had no idea why she was there, why Dorothee was, or what they were supposed to talk about.

—What is Ireland like for artists?

—You should ask one, Ute said.

—I thought the place was full of them?

—I've met a couple of local writers who seem to expend a lot of energy to ensure that they don't have to do any work.

—So speaks the perfect German. Can I mention something else?

—By all means.

—You have something about you. A creative spirit. I see myself in you.

Ute thought Dorothee was out of her mind. They went for a walk so that she could put more change in the parking metre, strolling along Grafton Street like the tourists they were. Dorothee just by being Dorothee was nothing but delightful. It was her job wherever she went to notice everything. All was precisely as it had ever been between them—one of them airy, the other in awe—except Dorothee continued in the intimate tone she had never used before today.

—It may surprise you to hear that I don't have that many friends.

The information was delivered as though Ute were being let in on a bargain. Beyond that, she could not fathom why Dorothee was so in need of a confidante. Of course, Ute would have paid good money to avoid the subject of her own loneliness. Did it seem strange that they made no mention of her parents? Not at the time.

Dorothee had no plans for the afternoon—nor, for that matter, had Ute—but, as they walked, they both seemed to turn inward and did not talk much at all. Neither of them had jobs to speak of, yet it was odd to be loafing around during work hours. Afternoons for Ute were the loneliest. So much of her life was spent having lunch with Tort, and then making love and quite quickly that turning into napping. For the want of anything else to say, she suggested they go to Brown Thomas. Between them, they probably possessed enough elixirs to stock a department store, but there were always errands to run.

Ute had to keep Dorothee from blitzing the place: a kimono with prancing animals on it, which she said Ute absolutely had to have. Of all the things Ute had expected to go home with, there wasn't one nice thing she could say about that kimono. She ended up sending it to Mama the following Christmas.

—Let me get you something small to pop in your bathroom cabinet.

—As long as it's small.

—As long as it comes in a box tied up in a ribbon.

—I have so much that I don't use.

—I've stopped working in the vines in the afternoon. Direct sun at my age is not good.

Ute fell for the image of Dorothee during a harvest. The great panorama of her farm in the Pfalz and the tender care taken with the sorting of the fruit, Dorothee carting the odd box herself, never yelling, never having to. The grower and her valuable land, her devoted team of workers, and her high-quality grapes. All the things Papa had never had.

—I'd love to hear more about the vineyard.

—I'd love to tell you.

Then Dorothee changed the subject, overdoing it in an attempt to be excited about moisturiser. It was no coincidence that they both liked the more expensive brands.

There was less sorrel than she had expected—Mama had put the doubt in her mind—and Ute marvelled at the viciousness with which her mother was scraping the cobbles, one after another, so that the sunlight, no longer absorbed by moss, was bouncing everywhere.

—I don't want you to be upset by what I said yesterday, Mama said. She had her back to Ute and was breaking up knotweed with a bread knife.

—I hate to think of you worrying.

—Impossible, Mama said. She had really weighed it up.

Ute ran more water over the yard and, eager to be finished, they worked without talking for another hour in a pleasant spell of productive companionship. The heat was thicker than in the morning, dissolving into humidity as the wind, scattering salsify seeds, promised another storm. She tore at a patch of stubborn dandelion before deciding with a victor's sigh that this would be the end of it for today. Perspiration was sheeting down her forehead and flooding her eyes,

Everyone was sweaty and Papa, who had been sitting on the bench, was particularly sodden. They had forgotten all about him. Mama got him upstairs and into the shower without too much fuss. In her parents' bedroom, Ute lowered the pulley from the ceiling, shushing the rope complaining on its descent. On it she found a formal white shirt that she hoped Papa would keep clean until Seanie came round this evening. She ironed it along with some proper trousers and laid them out on the bed with a flush of pride. All the ties she found were funeral ties.

Mama led Papa from the bathroom in an open dressing gown—the very picture of an abject prizefighter. After she had dried him and cajoled him into his underwear, Papa settled into an obligingly obedient sulk. Under his chest seemed to be a bustle of activity, as though under those spoke-like ribs a population of worms were going about their docile business. A kingdom of good that might have been keeping him alive.

Ute held up the shirt with the enthusiasm of someone about to dress her first corpse. Papa wasn't sulking, just making himself vacant so this demeaning episode could be over with.

—There's nearly a whole bag of salad downstairs, she said. I'll wash it and we'll have it for dinner before Seanie comes over. It's too hot for anything more involved than salad.

Then Papa surprised Ute by taking the shirt from her and putting it on, and buttoning it himself before swinging his legs into the trousers. It had never occurred to her that he could still dress himself. She must have regarded him with a mixture of tenderness and jealousy—when her day came, who would fetch the ice cubes?—along with a reassuring premonition that presumably her end would come about under this same roof.

The doorbell rang, an event in itself, since it sounded so electronic and modern. Ute hoped Seanie wasn't going to be early. She was sure to have half the garden in her hair and she was feeling rather scrambled after dealing with Papa.

Ute heard her mother say, —You're here?

With the emphasis on the you're.

The doorway shook and Ute shook with it. She didn't know what to say, because Tort was not in The Hide, he was here—standing outside until he would be invited in—and he was staring at her and it was unlike the countless times he had stared at her before.

She hadn't seen him in white trousers in so long, and some of the downstairs cuttings had caught on the hem. He had sweated so much that his blue shirt seemed patterned.

—Your mother's right, he said. I'm here.

Mama stood aside before finding a sudden urge to get back to work downstairs. Tort loomed large, of course, and the noon sun tucked itself obligingly behind him and the effect was of a halo.

The wrong man in the doorway in flames. Was all the work they had done that morning in preparation for his arrival? Her fear was that everything was as it seemed.

—I've landed right on top of you, he said.

—You have.

The shutters blew back and forth in the wind—the storm intending to ruin Tort's moment—and Ute gave him the job of securing all the windows. She felt suddenly protective of her parents and their house, which was too hot and suddenly had too many people in it, Ute included.

Tort had been up since four. She promised coffee then boiled the kettle for tea while discouraging him from speaking to Papa or from snooping—he was always into other people's things—or from calling out to Mama who, since the wind was getting up and scattering seeds, was rushing around to get everything, edible or not, into refuse sacks.

Tort followed as Ute checked on the bedroom. Papa was sitting on the bed where she left him, all the previous vigour long since departed. If he heard Tort's voice, he didn't acknowledge it.

—Don't worry, I'm staying at The Terraces. Right across the river from you. Maybe we could talk there.

—You're staying?

—It's not a day trip.

Ignoring her plea to stay put, as well as the tea it had taken her too long to make, Tort walked outside to sniff the air and compliment Mama on all the verdant aromas she had been personally manufacturing. One thing he didn't lack was manners, and he was soon downstairs helping her mother sweep up the cuttings before the rain came.

Ute settled Papa at the table with a new album—not 1939, for a change—and went to the bathroom to run water through her hair. There was grass in her mouth; she was a perfect scarecrow. She mopped at herself with a facecloth before having an idea, which in the circumstances seemed very daring indeed. She was uncomfortable about leaving Mama alone with Tort, but she couldn't imagine him doing much damage in the time it took her to take a shower.

The water was tepid but she turned the setting all the way to blue. And the moment Ute stepped into the little plastic shower tray and stood rigid under the cold needles, the day was again hers.

Ute returned to the kitchen just in time to miss the worst of the storm and the last of the sweeping. Mama left to take her own shower. It went without saying that she was hoping Tort would be gone by the time she returned.

Ute pictured the awful holiday they had all gone on. There'd been some vague plans to buy property in Majorca. Tort had assumed that Christa and Julius would only be too happy for him to sponsor their side of the trip, but Mama wouldn't entertain the idea, and wasn't interested in his attempts to persuade her. What Ute never warned him of—and what she supposed was still true—was that her mother thought that accepting another's hospitality created an economy of which she wanted no part. Without consulting anyone, Mama booked their own flights, and she reserved the most basic room the hotel had to offer, overlooking the carpark. Papa was more than happy with the room, just as he was happy to breakfast on the food they had brought from home. The cold meat kept perfectly well in the cool of the bathroom. It was bad enough for Tort to think of her parents doing without a view of the port, it was worse still to picture them eating perspiring meat off paper plates that they would rinse in the sink and hang outside with the towels.

On the second afternoon, Mama called to their attic suite and, declining the invitation to see the view from the terrace, asked to speak to her daughter in private. She had just been for a walk to the supermarket in Sóller town, and returned to find that someone had arranged for their belongings to be moved to a suite on the hotel's top floor. Tort was sure she wouldn't mind—the rooms were more or less the same, the new one was just a little bigger and higher up, with a terrace and, of course, a better view. What could be finer, he said, than cocktails on adjoining terraces? But Mama minded very much. That night at dinner, Mama and Papa spoke only in German, which made Tort progressively jittery and downright gloomy before he seemed to lose heart altogether.

The trip was otherwise uneventful, in that nobody said anything for the rest of the week. Her parents organised their own transfer to the airport. Life was so hectic—this was during the building of The Hide—that it took Ute another year to register that they weren't talking to her.

—The garden at home misses you, Tort said.

—I'm busy here, she said. As you can probably see.

Papa's eyelashes were beating very slowly in response to the conversation. Tort kept looking to catch his eye. Her father seemed hardly different this morning but Tort's presence had made him seem so much more pathetic—his arms skeletal against the white of his shirt. Her chest was pumping. The worms she had seen under Papa's chest were now squirming inside hers.

Quietly, she said, —What are you doing here?

Tort's bobbing knee was making the kitchen table and everything on it shake. Instead of answering the question he started to tidy the mess, listlessly moving everything around until he found himself with a stack of junk that intentionally or not obscured Papa from view.

—There was a system to that. Mama will be annoyed with you.

—Give her a reason for once.

—She wasn't annoyed before. Just busy.

—You can't be surprised to see me, he said.

—No, I am surprised, she said quickly.

It would have hardly mattered what he did, since she would have judged him for it anyway. She had always failed to acknowledge that his right to happiness was as great as anyone else's. And for this she was sorry.

—I'm soaked, he said.

—You can clean up at the hotel, I'm sure.

—Will you join me?

Ute glanced at her father, who was doing a good job of impersonating the shuttered window. She could have done with seeing the kind of proprietorial demeanour he used to reserve for Markus's visits.

—I expect you've booked the entire top floor.

Tort smiled, this wasn't that far from the truth.

—I'm happy to beg you to join me, he said.

He was wrestling with himself. She assumed his seething torso was from the effort for once not to transmit the worry that was escaping him everywhere. His throat had gone red in distress, as though he had been blanched in boiling water. There was a small puddle of sweat in his sternum and his shirt was entirely a different colour from when he'd arrived.

—There's so much I want to say to you it's making me choke. Someone could stick a tube down my throat, clear me out.

—Let's not, she said.

—I'm worried that anything I'm going to say will make things worse.

Worry was something you were as well coming to terms with. He was always pining for something, and being sorry about it, and he always meant it. At least he was being polite, and she was enjoying the conversation and her dominant role in it. She couldn't help laughing at the mess the rain had made of his trousers. They were as substantial as paper napkins. He reached for her hand and when she let him take it, just at that moment, if he'd asked to kiss her she would have let him.

His waking moment he mistook for coming to on top of a bonfire.

Fuck this, he thought.

And a fuck this was said to the outdoor tomb of Julius's vineyard.

Add to this some fairly fucking wild BO and the uncertain voltage of a hangover.

The river was barely there through the rye. Lizards underfoot, some as small as worms. The drama of a wild rose. Sunflowers? Ah, sunflowers. And, on its rounds, an officious bumblebee checking and forgetting, and double-checking again. As suggested by the bee, Seanie made an effort to settle. Clear lungs would be a boon in the circumstances.

He lay there in the clover, the oily air and fleshy rampancy, nettles tottering like stilt-walkers. Not for the first time the grass was whispering. The aroma was sweet and of paradise. Its effect on him was the motions of rapture leading to the thing itself.

The developments with Ute had to be considered. Were they proceeding to the stage where they could be called developments? Seanie's desire for her was the desire of a bee for a plain flower, or a field of stubble for fire. He'd fallen for her, and she for him; into the river, into Susanna's and out of it.

He took a whale-leap out of the grass then, heading down into town in preparation for the night ahead. There'd been a word with Andi at Les Insouciantes, seats reserved for Julius Pfeiffer plus guests.

From the hillside, the sounds of festivities multiplying. Allotments alive with gabbling and pork smoke and the gruff clamour of victory foretold. The divilment was infectious.

What was the percentage of Germans expecting the win? One hundred.

Momentum carried our hero over the bridge, busy as, with more appearing by the second. Behold shirts of the proud eras (1954, 1974, 1990) over bellies magnificent as gas tanks. Hawaiian leis in the appropriate white, black, yellow and red. A Stetson or two, painted the same.

On the bridge, he made a move for his favourite balcony to spark the last of the 9 Pound Hammer. He was looking for another dimension to the water. A few draws before flicking the joint into mid-air. The river was on fire, the river wasn't on fire, that kind of thing.

The next balcony along was occupied by a well-dressed couple, significant in their dimensions. He made out a shape, and as the shape was splitting it began to block the sun on him. Through surreal abstraction, the scene began to express itself: Ute in multiple exposure, a number of different rivers.

Like the path up to the vineyard, his mind was zigzagging, and his heart was, his heart was, his heart was. For it was everything he could do not to see the shape was making itself into the love part of love. Ute and one other.

The bridge might have collapsed from under him. He was considering whatever it took (a bed of feathers, a hook, a net) to keep him from the water.

Ute, his beautiful mountain, his blocker of the sun.

Seanie was just down from the hill, but the reserves of pastoral thoughts were running low. What was he to do but turn in on himself? The day had lost all its bounce.

It would have been a good time for Dad to make an appearance, and here he was now.

—She carries herself well, that one.

—She may have eluded me, Dad.

—That would seem to be the way the evidence is accruing. Are you sure this is all news?

—It is.

—Your mother was engaged to three different men when I first met her. It was a bit like buying a Lotto ticket, I wasn't proceeding with a great deal of certainty. A fella with a tool-hire, and not one but two Spaniards. If you were to consider my options, I was as well not bothering. But I would have done anything to put a crown on her head. Then nature played its hand. Was there anyone in the parish with cherry blossom in their yard? It turns out your mother was very susceptible to petals. And I had enough blossom scattered up the path that your grandmother called the corporation.

—I've no trees, what am I to do?

—We'll have to come back to that. This young woman was about to move to a village full of mad bastard Basques.

I had to have her in no doubt that there was a clear horizon before us. Come what may, there'd never be a harsh word, indoors or out. I got very excited in myself, and it was that bother that saved me. A bit of worry early on is like an inoculation, a polio jab. Things settled down a small bit after the wedding. We had our pleasure, the like of which keeps me going still. Do you care for snow sports at all? I've no notion if you do, but we'd our share of skiing holidays, like we were in *Hello* magazine. I had a fur coat, I was considering building a dry slope out the back of ours, I had the planning. And the light, is there anything as holy as a Dolomite at the break of dawn? You'd get a fine sunburn in winter, and often there were wolves in earshot. Then your mother had a scare on a chairlift, she was fine, no bones broken, and we never left Cloonfad again. It turns out the Donnellans are not skiing holiday people. It came time again for the petals and she'd no idea what she was in for with my tomatoes. Did I tell you about the time I grew peaches? I called them after your mother.

Les Insouciantes

Inasmuch as he treated anyone as an equal, Tort treated women as equals. His goodbye to Mama had been so vampish and risqué—the blown kiss—as to demonstrate that he revelled in being treated as an adversary and in not being taken seriously. With the hotel receptionist he was the same.

The Terraces faced the river from the north side, with each floor offering postcard-worthy views of the river and the altstadt—Bauamtsgaße was in there, behind the trees—and the schloß. There was a jacuzzi which, regarding them as inferior to sentō spas, he wouldn't use. Only the breeze gave the scene life.

The low-energy lighting had dissolved the edges of the space, and the last thing Ute saw before closing the curtains was the Sankt Hedwig. The room was dim and grey and the walls were moving, and she found herself in the mirror, having sex with the man with whom she had spent fifteen listless years, whose touch now seemed to her like old-fashioned electricity. She enjoyed it, there would have been no point in doing it otherwise, but every time they kissed, or whatever it was they were doing, there was an apparition of Seanie in the same reflection. All afternoon she had felt him looking right through her.

It was true that hotels made chaos of your mind. In this room, with its atmosphere of preoccupation, which in the act of love was indistinguishable from rancour, there was nothing about them to say that she and Tort were no longer lovers. For those few moments, that's what they were. One of them ascending, the other descending.

Tort was a cranky and demanding lover. She was required to give him her full attention. He lay there as she worked around him, seeming to take comfort in the procedural elements as much as the orgasm, which slipped out of him as a mist. Perhaps the scene was not that unusual, a brief pool of ecstasy that had no effect on the indifference surrounding it. Why this intensity—she refused to call it intimacy—was manifesting itself then was irrelevant, in that she couldn't answer the question. But, it was sudden and of course she knew that it was fleeting.

They had as usual been able to have sex without it being in any way sexual. Afterwards it took him half an hour to pee.

—Still going, he said. Pills.

He wanted them to shower together, which always meant one thing: Ute making do with the spray while Tort lathered and rinsed himself as slowly as he felt like, before drying himself with all the towels. When he left her alone in the shower, she was filled with a yearning to find Seanie and speak with him. Instead she heard Tort ordering room-service sandwiches to their usual specifications. Some kind of good manners had to be maintained. At least they would have behaved like adults.

She couldn't see her way clear to flee before consuming the food that had been ordered in her name. Guilt obviously made her hungry, and Ute had also asked for a packet of cigarettes and was going to smoke them one by one until she felt normal again.

—I didn't plan any of that, he said.

—Which part?

—Any of it.

—You bought a ticket. You got on a plane.

The sandwiches arrived, and Tort opened the curtains so they could see what they were eating. Birds chattered to express relief that the storm had moved on. Their entire continuum was being compressed into another penthouse where the luggage hadn't been placed on the rack or unpacked, and a water glass had been placed directly on the polished sideboard, and you were sure to trip over your own shoes—time-honoured signs that this was home for neither of them. Nothing but a rented room awaiting someone to do the rounds in advance of its next inhabitants. Honeymooners, perhaps. Ute and Tort had spent so many nights in bridal suites.

—Do you want to come over here to watch the match? If there are fireworks afterwards we'll be in the best place to see them.

—I have plans.

—Then I'll come to you. Home or out?

—I have plans.

With anguish that had to be equal to her own, he said, —Ute, no!

—I will be watching the football with Papa, my friend and Papa. I can't change my plans now. Papa has been looking forward to it all week.

Her blood was pumping faster than it had during sex. She stood and placed her sandwich on the tray. Tort looked suspicious, of the food Ute hadn't eaten and of her.

—You may as well eat that, she said.

—You'll be bowled over by this, but I'm not hungry.

Tort managed the sandwich anyway. Ute went out to the terrace to smoke, her hands shaking as though she had had a bad scare. Smoking was an indication that she'd let herself down. She couldn't abide the image: a woman, with the weight of the bloody world on her shoulders, smoking after sex. When Tort came outside he nudged her in the ribs to acknowledge it.

He found an ashtray and held it for her, to demonstrate that he was savouring the moment and his immaculate timing in rescuing a situation he had for once done little to bring about.

—Turner painted that view, he said. And Wilde's sons went to school next door.

He was displaying the kind of graciousness he reserved for business meetings.

—I'm going.

—You shouldn't be frightened of how much I love you.

—It's not that. You've seen Papa, how he is.

—Will I see you later? Will I?

—I don't know.

—If I ask you to marry me?

Tort accompanied this, as she bloody knew he would, with an absent look. A finisher of her sentences in any other conversation, why he always hesitated in the middle of asking her to marry him she would never know. Almost a proposal. And for a moment she was back under his spell. Their lonely house, her muffled being and the unreachable ladder to heaven.

A group of students dressed like travelling carpenters had descended from the Philosophers' Walk and were heading towards the old bridge. A switch had been flipped, and the night of the World Cup Final had begun.

Was this to be her lot? A bunch of drunk Bavarians and a marriage proposal from a cheerful man who had always treated her as if she was more compelling than any view and who always posed the question so companionably and hesitantly that it was as if she were being encouraged—no, depended upon—to defer an answer?

Leaving the bridge, she could see Tort's amber obelisk on the hotel terrace. She couldn't tell if he was there waiting for her to drop out of sight or if he was just there.

The electric fan Mama was holding was blowing her thin hair into little grey clouds. She was turning her head from side to side and smacking her lips as though she had just swallowed a cobweb. She smoothed her hair and stared straight into the fan's little plastic propellers. Her eyes were slits and her face was icily pale.

—Mine, she said to the fan.

—Are you stoned?

—Are *you*?

—I wouldn't have thought so.

—I don't want to talk about it, in case that's what's about to happen.

Ute guided Mama into the bedroom, where her mother approached the bed like a mechanic about to inspect a damaged bumper. Papa was lying on the other one and his shirt was soaking. Ute helped him out of it and searched for another. There was the polo shirt in which he'd have seemed too vulnerable—the short sleeves—so she decided on ironing the white shirt and somehow getting it back on him.

Then her father, buttoning his shirt, said, —You must be tired after all your work this morning.

The day had taken the right turn. Papa's comment, the first words he had spoken directly to her since she had come home, was quite irrelevant to her present situation, and just what she needed to hear.

—Not too tired at all, Papa. But thank you for asking.

She got him up and settled him in the kitchen before the TV. Football was a sport she didn't like and this week had been impossible to avoid—at the airport, on the streets and now, in the crowds pouring into the university quadrangle next door where they would be watching the final on a screen the size of a building.

Had it taken a football tournament being played many time zones away to strike her in the heart? The commentators on TV were going over the semi-final. One of them, a man wearing more jewellery than Ute, was trying to inflate the significance of Germany's win, against Brazil in Brazil, connecting it to a resurgence of national confidence, something Ute had never considered to be in short supply. All her life a German abroad, she had been adrift in the company of a certain type of compatriot: quietly happy in their lives, but send them abroad—and, most likely, give them more beer than they would drink at home—and they became different people, quick to complain about the variety of the hotel breakfast, the temperature of the hotel pool, the size of their towels. In other words, the rest of the world, though all well and good, was in need of some improvement.

The lid of summer was down, and there was the slow purr of a reckoning. In the yard, the haggard stalks and weeds scattered in rags. Up the stairs he went, ignoring anything to do with Hannah. The plan was, as far as plans went: have the one in Susanna's, and then to Les Insouciantes for the excitement of the big screen.

Julius was panting at the door, the tongue hanging out for the want of a drink. Ute was just out of the shower and he was lulled into thinking she was getting ready to join them. But the afternoon could be read on her (she was in and out herself, barely letting go of the breaths), and he knew then they weren't going anywhere together.

Now he was feeling worse, and the worse Seanie Donnellan felt the more cheerful he got.

—How are all the Pfeiffers this evening?

Destiny was laid out in these hopeless refrains. His eyes had to be singing.

—My mother's been smoking that stuff you gave her. She's just gone to bed.

—Make sure there's a bucket by the bed. And a big glass of water.

He felt a moment's warmth in her face as she said, —I will have to keep an eye on her.

—I was nearly thinking you might be joining us for the night.

—I'm a little tired, she said. But I thought you should know, I had a nice time last night.

He was as well not thinking about nice times, that there'd been any. The evening had gone very plain, and the grime of the passing days was cutting into him. Any line of thought he followed took him back to the shapes on the bridge. His beautiful mountain, his blocker of the sun.

He reached deep inside of himself to say, —Did you now?

—You're being very nice, taking Papa out.

—I told you I would.

—He could watch it on TV. We could all have a nice time here.

—I'm not sure we would. The head's hanging off him.

—You'll get him home safe and sound?

He waited for her to go on, but she didn't. He stood on the steps like he'd stood in the yard the night before, when he tried to remember the words of the poem and he couldn't, and he tried to decide what was worse (not being there, or being there with her like this, after that), and there was a sally of images from their day together. Her in mid-air, her skin against water, their feet under the table at Les Insouciantes, their feet drawing lines on the floor of Susanna's, all that Müller-Thurgau in the pair of them. The sad man's waltz.

The images invited another visitation, for these days our hero was very rarely alone.

Noel Donnellan was declaring himself an admirer of German vegetables. He had set himself a table in the yard and was sitting down to a dinner of tomatoes eaten plain as you like from a paper bag. He was trying to make a few things clear. Easy fucking does it with the trowel, son. Would you just stop itching at yourself? Julius has been put in his good shirt, you're his right-hand man, so stay mortal cool and whatever you do don't let him bite his tongue.

Dad's presence made one thing clear. There was hope in the night yet The night's mysteries might draw Ute back yet. By those means she might well pull up a chair just in time for the final whistle.

Ute was giving her father a hug. Julius hung his arms by his side, as if she was all the time at him for affection (this was not exactly characteristic behaviour), and Seanie was not above noticing that the old man was being sent out in his slippers.

She did her hair then sat with her head in her hands until it was all messed up again. She found a pair of shorts and a T-shirt in the German team colours. Today whoever she felt she was as German as anyone, of one kind or another at least, as well as the worst kind of false-hearted. Worst of all, Seanie—exactly on time, and still in the wrong clothes—had brought with him the smile that fed off itself. Only a few hours ago she would have professed his optimism as a kind of doctrine, but Tort's presence here in the first place was a challenge to which she responded with all her old bewilderment, no, foolishness.

Good God, she was fighting herself like a child.

Not only had her spell with Tort deflected the evening off its course, it meant that she and Seanie were not going to be. At least as far as the daydreams she'd had in Susanna's and this morning were concerned. He didn't say if he'd seen her anywhere around the place with Tort, but he must have done. It was in his eyes and in the pitch and tone of his voice and the fact that, with Papa, he couldn't be anything other than careful and so gentle.

She got undressed and stood under another cold shower until her throat ached and her teeth chattered. In her room, she lay on the bed without a towel so that the sheets soaked right through to the old mattress.

The thought—an image of Seanie watching her with Tort—presented itself with such clarity and forcefulness that it froze something in her. Even as Tort had stood in the kitchen door, she knew the day would go in a direction that would take them to bed. It was the worst thing she had ever done and what she could not bear to admit was that it took the thought of Seanie being humiliated before her feelings for him could take their full shape, before she allowed them to, and that she could only recognise love in juxtaposition with someone else's suffering.

The bells of Heiliggeistkirche were ringing a dashing tune. Football fans in high places. And the streets of the altstadt were squashed with frisky souls, a foxy load of young ones, their currents visible in the air and joy, all very well, secret in their hearts.

Hope explained the restiveness, the sassiness, and Julius, too, was verily cantering along the cobbles.

The clientele at Susanna's were no aficionados of sport, nor of much to do with this century, but all through the bar torsos straightened. The presence of Julius Pfeiffer was no everyday occurrence. Seanie got him settled on a stool with his feet swinging. Susanna's swivelling eyes became a stare, but Julius was customarily keeping things close to his chest, blithely accepting a glass of schnapps, and the chaser of warm Müller-Thurgau, itself chased with a small Pilsner and the side order of ice.

—On the house, Susanna said.

The wine was sipped with an immediate colour rising, the head on him like an old oxheart. Before Julius there also appeared a brötchen, inside of which was the legendary landslide of honey and butter, a sign that regal Susanna was on the move from sullen to slightly less sullen. Her bejewelled hands came to rest on his schnapps-bottle shoulders.

She spoke in dialect, along the lines of: it's good to see you, you old fool, where have you been I thought you'd died.

At the window, the crowds funnelled along Untere Straße. Divil and all bowling along to Marktplatz to get their fill. It was a powerful schlep to get Julius out of Susanna's reach and along to the terrace at Les Insouciantes.

There was a quiver to the animation, the mood in the square arrhythmically veering from impatience to soulful introspection. The bars with projectors proud as flags, the flags themselves tied to bicycles, around foreheads and to passing children.

No joke, but getting the old man to his seat was like guiding in an aircraft. Getting him seated at all was to be regarded a victory. Seemingly propelled by a blast from a heavy-handed sniper, Julius, with a holler of advance apology, pitched himself into someone's lap.

—Everyone is friends tonight, the woman said.

Julius commanded total respect. Some doing that took, thought Seanie, commanding almost none.

He knelt down to speak to the old man, reassurance being offered (the match, Germany, the big night), and Julius listening as though Seanie was an expert on such matters.

Andi, the barman more used to a slow afternoon with the paper, was making his finicky way through the tables. With meaningful eyes, he delivered a bottle of Sekt in an ice bucket.

—From Herr Tort.

Inside Les Insouciantes there was a reminiscence always of France. Belmondo and Platini on singed walls, the zinc of the bar agleam.

Dagmar was throwing a bucket through the ice drawer. A man in great swathes of linen leaned forward to partake in the cold mist. Everything was rumpled and damp, there was almost a rainbow coming off him. Then there was the slow-burning cigar. In puzzlement he studied the plume, curlicues of smoke bending to his will.

—A long time since I smelled one of them, Seanie said.

—How long exactly?

The voice was Irish and, wouldn't you know, belonged to the shape on the old bridge.

The taint of voice and bulk together: an overstuffed Lord-Lieutenant-type, jowls sheening in the heat, nose in a glass of something brown and apple-smelling. Seanie was no man to cast aspersions, but one thing he was prepared to say: this Tort fella had been doing the dog on the brandy. He was that bit purple.

—And you are?

—Friend of Ute's, Seanie said.

Tort quietened around a smile. A wink of deluxe smoke, and the gift of not giving a shit, not seeming to. Seanie saw them on the balcony on the bridge, their shape, and Ute fitting so closely around him.

—Upon my soul, Tort said.

The spicy larynx was always best avoided, but in that very moment Seanie was all for going fucking gorillas. Nothing showy, but a claw hammer in a man's skull would soon take their mind off the heat. Upon my soul.

A new roar billowed in from outside. Andi came in the door to collect a tray of cloud-covered Pilseners. The square was spilling over with hooting, trumpets twisting. Flugelhorns and bugles and fierce, metallic drums.

—You don't want to miss the anthems, Tort said.

The Argentinian anthem was a waltz and a squall. Between all the screens there was a split-second latency, and a haunted sound was carrying across the square. Andi ran back to catch his breath, puffed out from running table to table. His words were sucked into the night, and the noise of the people in the square, in the stadium, the reverb from all the televisions.

—Shout, Andi. You'll have to shout.

—He got confused. He thought you were gone.

Confused was right.

Andi hadn't a notion where Julius was. Tort heaved himself off his stool to follow Seanie outside. It took them half a second to establish that Julius was nowhere in view. The other half to estimate two thousand people in Marktplatz, their minds on things other than an old man probably halfway home to bed.

—He knows the way home, Tort said. Blessed old fool. It's five minutes away.

—He doesn't know a thing.

—I've known that man for fifteen years. I know what he's capable of.

—If you'd met him in the last year and a half you'd know he's capable of sitting down and taking a shite on the street.

Seanie made a circuit of the square. Scanning the ground, under tables, looking to find Julius's slippers among the soaked leis and confetti. He had to get the slippers out of his mind. The whole town was demented with the match, half of them crooked with drink. Even a waiter with a corkscrew assumed the intent and motive of threat.

The best thing to do would be to split up: one (Seanie) to go to the Pfeiffers' and the other (Tort) to go down to the river, just as a precaution.

Seanie ran to Bauamtsgaße, inhaling as he went the soft smell of his father (roses splendid in a July garden, Dad's eyes passing lovingly over blooms in the best of form), pelting on for fear he'd blub.

The police station resembled the changing rooms of a municipal swimming pool. The policeman's colour was suspiciously high. This Officer Keller had had such a heavy hand with aftershave that Ute could hardly breathe.

—We will hurry, he said, then went about the admin like he had all night. He wrote slowly and with a pencil, as though used to slip-ups.

Tort was encouraging Ute to use words like 'expedite' and 'accelerate'. Ute gave them all the places where Julius might have gone, but there was a problem when she was asked for a photograph. She had instead to describe her father. With what sounded like pride, she said he was wearing one of his good shirts.

Their first stop was the Philosophers' Walk, where Ute tried to get out of a still-moving car. One of their neighbours had set up a television on milk crates and everyone there was piling into sausages and beer from a bin of ice. According to the empties and the waywardness of the singing they'd been there all day and, it being the night of the final, they were on top of the world.

The vineyard was empty apart from Markus caught in the act of eating unripe grapes. The sleeping bag he sported as a scarf and the dreadlock that may well have doubled as a mattress imbued him with soldierly common sense. Any more perspicacity was masked by twilight. The wild odours were either of the earth or his own.

—Have you seen Papa?

Markus regarded the question with apparent wonder. His expression only changed when Tort stepped forward to take Ute's hand.

Markus consulted the air in front him before asking, —He your husband?

—No.

—Do you have one?

—No.

The answers didn't seem wrong or right, just neat and convenient in the circumstances. Tort piped up with, —That's under negotiation.

Tort went to relieve himself in the vines, and Markus waved Ute towards a view of the darkening roofs of the altstadt. She listened as he told her that as children they had played down there. A flex of his biceps recalled the afternoons when he had carried her home from school. All this was absorbed into a state of helplessness. She was unable to offer him the assistance he needed, although, in all likelihood he did not view his life in those terms. At least she could tell why he was rifling through the foliage. Now that the vines had grown older, they had come to resemble arthritic old men from whose arms hung the unripe grapes Markus wanted her to taste.

Ute held his hand to stop him picking any more.

—It's too soon for the fruit, she told him. Wait another month.

In the gloaming a squadron of small, green birds—Papa would have known their names, once—chattered among themselves to announce the end of the day. And Markus's hand in hers was much softer than she had expected. She had spent the afternoon in bed with Tort, but how long had it been since Markus had felt so much as a hand in his? Papa had offered him that apprenticeship, and what would have happened to each of them had he taken it?

This was what she had longed for: the chance to tell Markus that she was as free and as available to him as she was when she was eighteen.

She couldn't resist doing something that she supposed no one else had done since then. As though she was about to tell him a secret, she placed her cheek next to his, so that for once in their lives Markus could have made the first move. The look he gave her—with his bright, boy's eyes—as he let go of her hand, was of someone who hadn't in all those years learned a bloody thing.

Crowd noise roaring from the neighbouring allotments coincided with Tort's return.

—Are they applauding me? he said.

A deserted autobahn, and night falling in about thirty seconds flat. Ute was scouring the ditches for any sight of her father. She had presented it to Tort that Papa in his state of alarm might have made his way to Forst and the home of the Völker-Steins. It wasn't the time for long stories, but Julius once had a lover called Dorothee.

Ute reported this as if grappling with a new and difficult doctrine, information of a volatile nature.

—Why don't we phone? Tort said.

—Humour me, please.

—I don't think Julius has it in him to get this far. If that means anything.

—No.

—We could have phoned.

—You said.

Then she was silent, but perhaps not for the same reason as Tort, who professed to be tickled by the thought of Julius as this volcano of desire. The Julius Pfeiffer that Tort said he knew took no stock in people at all. A taciturn man in thrall to objects: glass and vines. It would have been easier to interest him in a new tractor than any lover.

—He's probably at home in bed right now. Tucked up beside Christa.

—Why do you answer questions that don't need answering?

—You need a little reassurance.

—Why?

—I don't know why.

—I think it would be better for Mama if he did die.

—He hasn't died.

—I don't know whether that's being cruel or realistic.

—Not mutually exclusive. Not necessarily.

There was no bargaining with Tort. He had been very firm when Seanie offered to help look for Julius. Do something useful, son, he said. Take the Beetle, it suits you. Tort had actually called Seanie 'son'. But there were not many people in the world with whom she was intimate enough to get upset. Perhaps Tort was the only one.

—I've been in a funny mood since this afternoon, she said.

—It's not your mood. It was quite an afternoon.

—You were the last person I expected to see today.

This had been no ordinary proposal, and, no matter what else was going on, he was becoming impatient for an answer. It wasn't like Tort to hold his tongue—discretion whenever he showed it had to be accidental—and this was a weak moment and he was surely going to capitalise on it.

No, it seemed to be a time for tact.

Tort stayed silent and, by the time they came off the motorway, the atmosphere in the car was turning towards cordial and circumspect.

—Let's see where Julius has gone to, shall we? he said. The rascal.

With its narrow lanes and old stone glinting, Forst hinted at discernment and its own form of tact. Figs thrived here, marigolds appeared to grow like weeds, and the streets were lit as if in preparation for a medieval banquet. How on earth would they find anyone at this time of night? She hoped the Völker-Steins had some torches.

Tort piloted the BMW across the cobbles, commenting on the enormous manor house with few rooms occupied or lit. The overfed pansies and fussy shutters, even in the fading light, the colour scheme frantic-seeming. Having more of everything was one of the joys of being rich, she supposed.

—I had a nice time today, she said. This afternoon.

—That makes two of us.

—This would have been impossible without you.

—One thing I have going for me is my willingness to drive anywhere at the drop of a hat.

There was nothing much to see, nothing but purple richness, a mess of pale stars beginning to cast a glow over the labyrinth of vines. Tort's hairy, fat hand on the ignition key as he said, —You've at least considered my proposal?

He spoke as if he had tried not to put it as a question. All the reasons she had ever given him: children, not children, her grandfather—they weren't the right things to say, they weren't accurate. If only Tort had spoken to as her he did to everyone else, as though she was his employee, then the answer might have been yes. What she really wanted to say was that she might marry him one day. She could marry him, she thought. She could marry him, if she really wanted to.

The vines ran almost to the back door of the Stein house, from where she heard a haunted roar—something of significance in the football. Once Ute had grown used to the darkness, which was much less oppressive than at The Hide, she could sense things: a hissing sound, the plants imbibing what moisture they could and, somewhere, the sound of a mole-like animal ransacking the earth.

A breeze flushed the leaves, a reminder of the sweetness of the Neckar, carrying with it thoughts of her father, for whom she could do very little now. The closeness of the day was drifting off, and the effect of the fresh air was to suspend her in the moment. For now she could recognise—what it didn't help to—that loneliness had toughened her heart. She was shivering; and longing for her parents as never before, and feeling apart from them and weak without them, much weaker than before.

Hannah was sussing him out like he'd been trying to get away without paying a toll.

—I've seen you coming and going, she said.

—Been helping out with Julius.

—It looks like you're his nurse.

—More his right-hand man.

With these words, and the thought of an old man lying dead in the sludge of the river, the colour of the night ran from golden to bilious.

There'd been a call from Ute. Nothing doing up on the hill, so she and Tort were on their way to Forst. Someone had the bright idea that Seanie should take the Beetle up to the hostel in Wilhelmsfeld.

—You haven't been by for your bags, Hannah said.

—There's not much to get.

—Where have you been staying?

—Around.

—I had a feeling you'd go to Ireland.

—I'm here. But I wasn't keen on shelling out on a guesthouse, so it's been a sleeping-under-the-stars situation.

—Say you're not sleeping in the street.

—After a fashion, he said.

Stick to forty, Hannah was saying, but how could they stick to forty? And why and how the fuck had he asked her to come along? That he'd made a mistake was obvious to them both.

Once upon a time, she hadn't seemed to mind that Seanie was a grown man with three pairs of underpants, but then she had. There'd been frequent but always offhand talk of a wedding, summer or spring, but no final decision was ever come to. What came back to him now was a picture of helplessness, an image of a small boy tackling a rhino. For there was never sex without love for Seanie Donnellan, nor much interest in love without sex.

He held tightly to the wheel. All there was to know was within its circumference. They made their way upwards, the silent rebuke of the river at their backs. The balminess of the night the one thing droning them up towards the old hostel. But either the mountain or the car was tilting, and the Beetle was dying to roll back downhill.

A stray dog was the only other traffic on the road. A jittery pointer, ecstatic in freedom, the animal pale in the rolling light and its maritime effect. A roar came from one of the houses and, as if being dragged away by the shockwaves of an explosion, the dog veered off the road. Only a mad animal would think being driven at was a game.

Seanie got all Hannah's news. She was thinking of spending two grand on a modular sofa. She had seventeen days' holiday left after Greece. And, this week a mouse in her lab was born with elongated ears, which meant it had the right mother and the wrong father, or the right father and the wrong mother. The mouse wasn't so deformed that she would have been allowed to kill it, so they had to go through the rigmarole of sending its tail for sequencing. But there wasn't much worth analysing when a mouse was born with the wrong ears. She knew it as soon as she saw it and that it had been her fault.

—Anybody's fault but the poor little mouse?

—They aren't that choosy when it comes to lovers, she said.

There was an almighty session going on in the hostel refectory. The fella who came out to them, a brute in combat shorts and an eagle tattooed on his leg, was the bulb off yer man in *The Fast and the Furious*.

He was holding a set of bath taps but with the magic words (Julius Pfeiffer) they got fucked into a bush.

With arms folded, he said, —Lothar Pfeiffer?

Seanie, in search of peace of mind, rambled on about wild roses. But the niceties were against his instincts, and poisonous in the gob. There was fuck-all this brute knew about flowers. He was an aficionado of anything to do with Dr Lothar Pfeiffer. He wanted them to know the story of the house. In a whisper, he had this to confide: with the cheap labour available after the first war, the house was built by Julius's father and uncles and grandfather. Lothar Pfeiffer, for one, wanted to ensure a first-class childhood for his favoured son. The Pfeiffers summer-holidayed quare serious. Every day a fair-sized country wedding, three to five bottles of Mosel wine for the men, the children playing all the livelong day.

Seanie was a small bit ruffled. —We're as well to clear up a few things, he said. War talk does nothing for me.

A cry from inside suggested imminent assault. The TV was up so loud it rattled, and the air was expanding and collapsing. Someone in a white jersey had toe-bogged Germany into history.

With the goal came a sudden change in the atmosphere. The air became molten with roars of songs and folklore spew.

Out they all came, with their bitching leg tattoos, singing their classics: Comrades of the Golden Dawn. Snakes In the Woodpile. Maidens and Martyrs. Elves. Water Spirits. Tricksters. Blood Libel. Rhine Nymphs. The Story of a Boy Who Went Forth to Learn Fear. The Maid Freed from the Gallows. The Rotten Bones Are Trembling.

Optimism was lethal in the wrong hands.

An elderly farmer stood smoking against his gate, a life Seanie envied and might one day imitate. The man raised an arm at the rolling car, shaking his head, biting back questions, the earth moving and taking with it his last scrap of wonder.

There was a new fineness to the sky above the Holy Mountain. The stars making themselves understood on such a triumphant night. The Beetle rolled down towards town, Seanie steering more than driving.

Soon Heidelberg was upon them, and a quick little oh fuck at the sight of the roadblock on the bridge at Ziegelhausen. Silent sirens, spooky blue and sad red. Exactly what to do when you win the World Cup, breathalyse everything in sight. A call came in then from home.

—You'd almost say they deserved it in the end.

—The goal looked like a fluke to me.

—You saw it then. You don't sound like you were watching it.

—What would that sound like?

—I was saying to myself all along, extra time was in the breeze. I was even going as far as saying penalties.

—That wouldn't have been fair on anyone.

—You'd want to have a word with yourself for even considering fairness in this day and age. And look at them on their lap of honour. They're still running moves, some of them. You can take the rest of the night off, lads. Have a tin of beer, take it from the fridge you brought with you.

—Am I distracting you from it?

—You're no distraction, but I'll let you go. Can you imagine if they'd lost? They'd be going door to door looking for someone to take it out on. You'd be dragged along the cobbles for yourself. Victory is a different order. That's for the people, they'll be going buck fucking mental. Here come the good times. Listen to me, no nonsense out of you.

Passing through the roadblock, Seanie spoke aloud his heart to the night.

Soon they would learn Julius's fate, and football or no football the day's miseries and fears were all about them. The desperation was brutal but it was a trifle compared to the thoughts of Julius quicksmart under a bus somewhere. An *x* on a mortuary list, in paradise or on the way. Soul in repose and the football raging.

He shifted his hands on the wheel. He thought for a second that he might share a soft word, but he felt them to be long gone to the mountain now. He'd felt Hannah going when she'd look sideways at the way he buttered toast, and even then he'd had to limit the thinking, which was all too easily emboldened. And he'd known her to be gone when, across deck at the cruise ship, Hannah with two or three strokes accomplished a length of the Akropolis's tiny pool, her blistered shoulders doing the work necessary to carry her all the way away from him.

But it was Ute's presence that was coming to him now. The pictures newly made, and felt with urgency.

Up on the schloß people were lighting and launching victory fireworks. Smoke hung in the air, the metallic breeze coalescing with the sour odours of the celebratory Sekt, most of which had soaked the cobbles of Marktplatz. The pumps at Les Insouciantes had been left unattended. Overcome men who Ute wasn't sure she recognised from the other night at Susanna's or from her childhood began to sing a melancholic schlager, something better suited to a night on the après-ski.

The song—something about eternity, a vivid and confusing throwback to her teenage years—seemed incomplete without a wind machine. It wasn't a bad effort, she thought, for music no one admitted to listening to any more yet everyone seemed to know.

She was suddenly certain that Papa must have gone to the toilet in Les Insouciantes and had had an accident there—a fall on the steps. Tort indulged her when she asked him to take a look. As she waited for him, it occurred to Ute that the trip to Forst had been wholly unnecessary but necessary to her. Perhaps it had been important to see where Dorothee Völker-Stein used to live.

The atmosphere in the house had to have changed in the years since Dorothee had left for Scotland. But whoever had decorated the living room, which was about the size of the barn next door, had done so without a thought to what went with what—green, blue, pink sofas, new art in old frames, a piano that was meant for playing, one that wasn't, a cherry tree growing up through the tiles in the kitchen.

Ute was hypnotised by Dorothee still, and had behaved in the most offhand manner, as if Papa disappearing was a daily occurrence, and her real reason for travelling to Forst in the middle of the World Cup Final was to pay her respects to a woman who'd been gone for years, and who might as well have been, say, in the conservatory, cutting delphiniums and arranging them as only Dorothee could, for which Ute would have been more than eager to express admiration.

Felix Stein, by way of reciprocation, had been as nonplussed as the day before on the Sankt Hedwig. He didn't seem to mind if Ute stayed for a glass of Cuvée Dorothee or turned around and went out the way she came in. But he was alone, and Germany had just won the football. So he was prepared to field Ute's questions—the way she imagined he tolerated the locals who came to the cellar door for the five per cent discount on the wine—even though he seemed to know exactly who she was and, for that reason, would rather not have had to pacify her with polite talk of her father.

Papa wasn't there, and would never have gone there anyway. Ute would have been better off waiting for him in Les Insouciantes, which, Seanie or no Seanie, was all she had wanted to do tonight.

A wayward conga line exited one of the hard-rock bars along from Susanna's. The members of the conga, young men and women with no thought of the work they would have to get up for, were choreographing to music from multiple sources, a palimpsest of choruses—more pain-soaked schlager, Nina Hagen, some U2, some a-ha. Another more erratic conga swung out from Dreikönigstraße and headed in the direction of the original conga and, in one of the silliest things Ute could ever recall seeing, both of them observed the rules of the road by adjusting course to drive on the right.

As they started towards the river and home, everyone in the crowd, accidentally or due to trial and error, found the same song to sing—'The Final Countdown', another one from her youth whose words Ute took satisfaction in remembering.

She turned to Tort, saying, —I'm glad you were here tonight.

—I understand why you're upset at me. I know what it's like when you feel crowded. I crowded you. In a perfect world I wouldn't have. Even when I have the patience to wait, my curiosity gets the better of me. You should know that it's curiosity, not impatience. But I will give you as long as you need. I mean to say, don't worry, don't think too much about it, don't let it get in the way of the thing that is more important right now.

—Which you're keeping me from.

—There isn't much I can say to that.

—I don't want you to say anything.

—Right you are.

—I don't want you to say anything.

Tort kissed his fingers, and with his pinkie and thumb mimed a phone call. And then he was gone, to the old bridge and another penthouse.

The sound of celebrations was growing faint, but 'The Final Countdown' refused to fade. Ute fell in behind a group of women, her age and younger, wearing leis in the German colours. There were dabs of red, black and yellow on their cheeks. They were all singing but Ute discerned one voice in particular that made her feel loose and more hopeful, as though tonight's purpose had been not for Ute to misplace her father but to hear this song from her childhood sung so waywardly and with such purity.

The night was not lost, it was not lost at all.

There was also the possibility that this young woman always sang when she was drunk and—happy, sad or bored—she just happened to have a beautiful voice. Ute would have liked to have found a way to be more tender, but there had to be a way to bring more tenderness into the world without having to make a show of yourself in the street.

Whenever she and Tort saw each other again, life would be simpler than it had been. For she would like to have found a way to have been softer, and better at love. And she pictured him at home, in the spa as ever, his curious tongue chasing an elusive droplet of sweat—a bubble before it is blown. Inasmuch as their relationship was over, and this may have been the first time she had ever considered that, she understood that she had shared something with Tort: possibly not love, but something harder to manage and possibly more worthwhile.

Praise Not the Day until Evening Has Come

Expensive-looking moonbeams on the Neckar. The river was silver, the water polite. But the moment halved then and Seanie was best out of the car for this bit.

Julius was after being pulled out of the water.

He was half the size he'd once have been, yet still it was as if they were taking down an old statue.

The doughty man red in the face, the look in his child's eyes was pure disaster, they were looking from the other side of death. The dicey look on him and the pins all bare and bandy. Julius gave Seanie the nod then, daresay he'd home on the mind.

Time for Hannah to return the favour, and make herself scarce.

Seanie had a word with the ambulance nurse. The mirthless report of this a hotspot for suiciders, lone and dedicated, pegging themselves into the water you wouldn't know how often. It was a sorry old story and sure enough it was some job to survive a fall like that.

The nurse knew Julius, and he seemed to know her. She tried to get him covered in one of those things they give to marathon runners, but they would have needed a tarp to cover him properly.

A mug warm in Julius's paw. A cup of tea and he'd be unstoppable. With a great deftness to her movements, the nurse adjusted his head. She pressed her lips to his forehead and the years went by in two minutes, three. He'd had his tea but there was no moving him. For Julius was in the mood to talk.

He was all night trying to die, the water was supposed to smash like glass and he was supposed to break with it. He had planned to roll in front of a car but there were no cars. He waited to be mugged, but there were no muggers. The emptiness of the river, the height of the water, the stillness of the air seemed to promise a sweet and slowly darkening evening in which to stroll. But what on earth did the people of the town have to be excitable about? There'd been an almighty roar from somewhere, but it came from inside of him, and Julius was pleased to find himself somewhere else. At five years old he knew enough about life to act impressed by all the important visitors to the summer house.

Vati was always looking forward to something coming into flower or fruit. The woolly spikes of the edelweiss were seen as a sign. Leontopodium alpinum, Vati said. The best people knew Latin, and Julius, being interested in that kind of thing, should have known that already. So far, he knew plants by their colours and leaves, hairy and smooth, and not by their names. But Vati reserved the greatest anticipation for the walnuts.

The harvest sounded like a lot of work, but it would be worth it when everyone was eating toasted walnuts on Christmas Eve. He would shake the tree and gather a proud crop of nuts in the blanket they were picnicking off now. Julius would be allowed to open each one with his father's trusty pocket knife, and over the autumn they would lay them in the attic to dry. So it didn't make sense that Vati was somewhere else during his own harvest. More than anything Julius wanted his father to be there. Together, he and Mutti did their best to shake the trees, but nothing fell. They shook them so hard that Julius felt queasy and confused. He kept slowing down but Mutti kept speeding up. After an hour of shaking, a single walnut fell onto the grass. Julius took it with him and went inside. The hull wasn't nutty-looking at all. Later Mutti came into the kitchen with a box of green things she had picked on her own. They should have waited for them to dry but Julius couldn't wait. Vati had shown him a picture of a human brain in a medical textbook and Julius gave a cry of recognition when Mutti cracked the first shell.

There it was: a brain you could eat.

That night he was going to open the rest of them himself, one by one if need be, and dry them with a candle. After dinner, Mutti sewed as usual. There was nothing Julius could think of to occupy himself, and nothing that he could have done because he was so pent up. He poured his own bedtime milk and trooped upstairs with it.

It was late by the time Mutti turned off her light. Julius waited until he knew she would be sound asleep before creeping downstairs with a candle dappling the landing. He considered using a hammer and chisel to open the nuts. Vati had always been fascinated by matches and fire, and Julius thought to burn away the hulls. The house in Heidelberg had electricity but they used gaslight in the hills, and he came up with an excellent shortcut. So easy to make a bigger flame by holding the candle to the lamp. Hardly had he lifted the candle and there was the noise like the starting of a propeller. The lamp whacked the concrete floor and nuts tumbled everywhere.

The kitchen took easily to fire. He would hear that about wooden houses.

Julius crawled outside. He might have tried to drag the box of nuts out into the yard with him but his arm was already blistering. He had his head lowered when Mutti came outside, vampirish in the dark. He couldn't see her face but she was calm for someone who had fought through thick smoke. He could feel them standing apart as ragged flames, a ghost train's illuminations, spilt from the kitchen window. Mutti pulled Julius away and slapped him. One of the neighbours ran for the fire brigade, but they took ages to come all the way up the hill from the town.

What took them so long Mutti would never know, since this was known to be the house of Dr Lothar Pfeiffer. The firemen stood and watched as though they had never seen a fire before. The house survived, someone else lived there now, but at one point it looked like it might topple into the yard.

More tea, just a sip, for Julius, but not tonight the shoals. Gently the nurse lowed to him.

What had he in mind at all with the wandering off?

Calling to mind Speer and the Laureate striding their way home, the nature of which, at this stage in the game, had to be a vague enough picture. The ultimate destination a secret into the bargain.

There was a bit more messing before they got him to his feet for another mosey, traversing the ambulance's width and underneath him the path for once coming smooth.

A drowsy wind pushed the water upstream. The Sankt Hedwig was listing gently, and she was happy to think that it was being borne her way. The river was its most beautiful at this time of night, lacquered and settled in its indifference to everything that passed by and looked on.

She didn't know if she saw smoke above Papa's vineyard or not. The swirl in the sky seemed computer-generated and suggested Markus's presence on the hill. She wasn't sure how often he went there, if he went as often as Mama said, or at all.

Tiredness was coming in like something from a blunt instrument, but she heaved herself over the bridge and up the path to him.

The gate to the vineyard shouldn't have been swinging open—only Markus would move through long grass while trying not to disturb it. He bit the air as he walked, but began to watch his step as soon as he noticed her there. He may have been shaking for some time and he was shaking now. The row of vines he had just ruffled was manic with insects, inexhaustible even after a night spent ravaging one another. The day was dissolving into itself.

Markus, for once, had time for her. He still stood upright in his shirtsleeves, presenting himself for inspection. She circled him in her most commanding way. Her small boy who had become this big man with the permanent look of surprise at being trapped in the body of a beast.

How she wanted him to come home with her, for a bath, nothing more than a good scrub.

Having passed muster, Markus moved back towards the cabin. It had been tidied and prepared for someone's arrival. The glass was smeared with charcoal but he had tried to clean it, and he had draped a sheet over the pieces of Papa's old basket press. Some wildflowers were hung on it to dry.

He had a packet of chocolate biscuits and he sat down to eat them with his knees pressed together.

—Can I have one? she said.

He shook his head. He had been drawing, and no one could ever have accused Markus Kaltwasser of moving on too quickly from an idea. As far as she could see, it was dozens of versions of the same subject: a football player from their old team. It was nobody very real, just someone Markus liked to imagine to help him pass the time. He took her through the drawings one by one. The rolling wave he made with his hands suggested that everything the player did was automatic and of his own accord. The player didn't train, he prepared only as much as he needed to, and then he played.

In one picture, the player was uttering a private prayer—for the greater glory of God—and smiling to himself as he prayed. Concentration came from ignoring all the things at hand. There was a lovely one of him gathering the ball after he'd scored, one of him blessing himself and looking up into the crowd, one of him peeling past an indignant defender, and another in which he was floating like a gymnast's ribbon past raised studs, evading elbows as though they were meaningless chatter.

There was no doubt in Markus's mind that tonight the goals were going to come. If the player didn't score the goals himself he would make them and if he didn't make them he would create the space for those who did.

—Everything is automatic, he said.

Ute was less hypnotised by the pictures than made faint. It was ridiculous to be thinking of desire for Markus, but she registered it as that. He went to sit in a deckchair, facing downwards like he was staring into a stream. He removed his boots and socks, for there was poetry to be found in his own toenails. A peculiar thing to do, in the circumstances, but what man alone wasn't allowed to do peculiar things?

—I have to be off, she said.

—See you tomorrow, he said.

She was not even there, was she? Or her presence was troubling him. Tonight his hadn't troubled her at all, it had thrilled her as much as seeing the wild deer in the Valepp. For hadn't they been first to behold one another, and the first to be lost? They were not so old as to disregard the future, but it was not this morning's future, it was a new one in a world full of different people but not so many that, if Markus ever needed her, he would be able to find her.

The ashtray was beside the bed. Her mother was sitting with her knees tucked into her chest. Ute was less inclined to hold her tongue at this time of night, not an hour she was used to breezing in at. To look at her in any light, Mama was transparent enough to have been projected from a lantern slide.

—I think you're smoking too much, Mama.

—Do you think that?

—How often do you smoke?

—Friday night.

—Today was Sunday.

—And when I feel like it.

The bedroom was unnervingly blue, and Mama, in the light and as never before, seemed like a person at risk. Her skin was parchment-like, and her eyes were seething, and clear enough for Ute to see all the worry that would not be resolved by Papa's safe return.

—What if you pull back a little?

—Why would I do that?

—It's not good to lose control. If you could have seen yourself.

—But I like it.

—To not know where you are?

—Is that not the point?

—It's bad for you and it's illegal and there will be police coming, in one way or another, and I think you should stop.

—Why would I do that, when I like it?

—In that case, I can't be here if you're going to keep doing it.

—That's completely up to you, Mama said.

What Mama meant was: is this what you want to talk about now? So often their arguments lasted until morning, or for years, but it had been a long night for everyone and her mother had been home alone for hours.

Ute decided she would change Papa's bed. It made sense to do it when he wasn't there to get in the way. It still surprised her that he hadn't showed up downstairs, as if for work. She imagined him in the stained-glass light. No, he had cut glass all his life and his working days were over. Her father had worked too hard, she thought, never taking many holidays. Taking his dinner outside in the yard before a trip to the Philosophers' Walk was more than enough, he always said. The combination of working indoors and out made him a lucky man—that and the picnic for his friends every June, with no one eating the spicy sausages so they could enjoy the new wine.

Poor Papa. If she hadn't left him alone with Seanie he never would have walked off.

Poor Papa, he wouldn't have made it far.

—You like to choose your moments to attack someone, Mama said, examining her nails before turning them down out of sight.

—You should sleep. I'll wake you if there's anything to talk about.

Mama, a nurse and bloody-minded to her core, watched Ute strip the sheets. Since she was sure to be graded for her work, Ute was careful to approximate examination conditions. It was a surprise to find a dry mattress-pad, the sheets starched as solid as newspapers. On went the bottom sheet, the corners triangle-folded and mitred. She made sure the sheet was tight and wrinkle-free.

—You could consider fitted sheets, Ute said.

—Are we not civilised people? I could change a bed while someone was still sleeping in it.

Mama gave a smile of appreciation when Ute was finished with the top sheet, leaving it untucked so that Papa could easily get into bed when he got home. Ute gave a pillow to her mother to change the case, but Mama buried her face in it and wouldn't budge. Ute sat on the bed, the better to see Mama's expression. Her mother, of course, turned on her side and faced the other way. She waved her hand to suggest that Ute should busy herself elsewhere.

Ute had never been sick in her life—not so much as a hot lemon—and she was unfamiliar with the tricks of the bedside. Did you hold hands? Were you allowed to sleep in the chair? Ute didn't think she would be able to.

—Do you want some water?

—I know where to find the tap.

Mama had her feet outside of the sheet, and she waggled them. Her toes were stalky and almost as long as her fingers. They were the most expressive part of her.

Ute couldn't help but get into the bed. Mama seemed amused at the fact that someone would actually do that, but she arranged her shoulders in an exaggerated slump—it seemed to matter that Ute had sat on the corner of the pillow. Having made a show of getting into it, Ute felt obliged to stay there for a moment. Moments later Mama, her chest soaked with the night's hot exertions, her ribs as substantial as a quail's, was an awkward bundle asleep in the crook of Ute's arm. She was moaning a little, softer and lighter than usual—the effort of snoring too much for her. The sound was of water in the back of her throat. Her eyes were twitching, in a dream.

Ute moved in the bed. She didn't suppose her mother could feel anything, but Mama woke up, looking at Ute then up at the ceiling, dismayed to have had someone watching her sleep. She laid her hands on the cover with her palms turned upwards. Ute held out her forefinger for her mother to squeeze, but Mama ignored it, and the silly finger was stuck there, pointing.

—I'll get you something clean to wear, Ute said.

It took her a little while to excavate the drawers. No matter how many times she checked, all she found were scarves with their labels still attached that she had never seen Mama wear and didn't know she owned. Ute bet that her mother usually slept in that day's clothes anyway. Then she saw the polo shirt she had decided against for Papa and she remembered that for some reason she had sent him out in his slippers.

—Arms up, Mama, she said.

Her mother obliged her with one arm and Ute lifted the other, but the nightie was stuck to Mama's back and didn't want to come off. The cotton was so thin and old that Ute could barely get it off her without tearing it. She handed over the polo shirt and Mama put it on. Ute tugged it down and popped up the collar.

—Better?

Mama flattened the collar and got up to leave the room.

Having just left her mother's bed, Ute got into Papa's, even though she wouldn't sleep now. She undressed in the sitting position, like some invalid Mama would have had to work around. No, she thought, there must be something I can put on.

She got out of bed, went to the chest of drawers and searched through it, thinking for a moment that she might find the kimono Dorothee had bought for her in Dublin. It had vanished—of course—but there were all those other scarves in tissue smelling of lavender. Ute looked through them.

Since it was sure to be another warm day, she chose one with a picture of two flamingos in a nuptial parade, surrounded by palms, orange trees, tropical flowers. The scarf wouldn't be hers to keep—Mama was far too watchful for that—but Ute was grateful for the use of it anyway, as well as everything else she had borrowed. She unfolded it and went to drape it around her shoulders but the scarf was so light that, in hanging in the air before landing on her, she couldn't tell what was silk and what was breeze.

From the kitchen window, the yard had an embarrassed look to it—a few louche weeds they had missed the day before. There was the sound of the early bells from the Heiliggeistkirche. Papa wasn't home yet and the morning was sure to come with bad news, and so wasn't to be acknowledged.

Ute watched her mother peel some eggs with shaking hands, marvelling that she could do so when they were still blazing hot. Mama was able to remove them so deftly that the smooth pieces of eggshell could have been used to tile a bathroom.

Mama asked if she'd like something to eat and Ute shook her head, thinking how it would be a nice idea to eat breakfast with her mother, but she couldn't eat anything now. She checked her phone for messages as she had done two minutes ago and she made sure the landline was still in its cradle.

Mama had sat herself at the table but she got up to fetch the salt and pepper in case Ute changed her mind about the egg. The eggshells were dark tan, like the hen's owner, and the colour of the yolks was different from the eggs in Ireland, brighter and better.

—I don't know why anyone would consider themselves too good to eat breakfast.

—I have news for you. I eat breakfast.

—I didn't mean you, necessarily.

Ute sat at the table alongside her mother and took her hand, but Mama deemed two hands necessary to peel and eat an egg. They sat there for two minutes, exactly, with the dawn light starting to appear as relief and a reproach.

—You need a haircut, Mama said.

—I had one just before I came.

—A proper haircut.

—I'd prefer a night's sleep.

—I do it to myself.

—I've seen that.

Mama laughed, and how she moved—suddenly purposeful in a way that suggested the idea of cutting Ute's hair had not just occurred to her.

The clippers sounded tired. While Mama figured them out, Ute sat numbly with her chin on her chest and her eyes closed. The floor was warm under her feet.

—What will you say to him when he comes? I just want to know where he is.

—That's the wrong question, Mama said. It's impolite to ask someone where they've been when they don't know. It's impolite to ask questions people can't answer.

—I understand.

—I don't think you do.

As Mama untangled the strands of hair that had come to annoy Ute so much, an understanding grew thick between them—in this act, they could escape one another.

For Ute had never told Mama, even though it was the fantasy of most children, that as a girl she had actually prayed for different parents, a different father to be precise, one who wasn't called Pfeiffer. She had prayed for this to be so and the world hadn't answered her prayers and she prayed anyway. She couldn't say that whenever she was approaching a moment of happiness—an orgasm, say, or a joke or a dance—she could feel her family pulling her back to earth. She couldn't tell her mother that often she said she had no family at all. She would get around to it one day, she would say that she no longer felt any of this to be true.

Over the clippers' groan, Mama said, —I wish I was out there.

—You instead of Papa?

—As well as him.

—Is this because of someone in particular?

—I don't want to hear the name.

The last time Ute had seen Dorothee was before she had departed to save the artists of Scotland. Papa's retirement party, as Ute could remember it, had not been much of an event. He had not wanted to retire at all, but the insurance company had refused to provide any more cover for him. No one throws a party for losing their insurance, do they? he said. But Dorothee had made a show of inviting them to the Sankt Hedwig.

Mama had needed persuading to go, but Papa wanted to go for the dinner. It was goose season, and did anyone know how much geese cost?

The kick of being in the same room as dutiful Mama and exotic Dorothee. Even then, Ute understood the fascination, the caress of a high-octane power line. There were qualities, if she was to consider Dorothee, about which she was still curious. How, as a girl, she'd physically ache whenever Dorothee spoke, coolly and genially, the melody suggesting life was to be lived in a trance. And her indescribable smell, which Ute continued to crave. Not in years had it occurred to Mama to wear perfume.

Dorothee had on a floor-length dress coat, and Ute could see that underneath it there was a pair of silk pyjamas. The thought that she was being given the once-over made Ute nervous. Time and again she had daydreamed about presenting herself, as an adult, for this woman's approval—sometimes getting it and sometimes not. If she put her mind to it, she could have pictured every outfit this woman had ever worn. Dorothee no longer wore those Zuni bracelets, yet she rolled her wrists as though she was sporting something heavy. Her fingers were curled with arthritis. Perhaps the memory of jewellery was enough.

Papa said some thanks for the goose and started to eat, at which Felix—relief and annoyance being the same thing in his world—gave a childish sigh. He faced the gathering with arms folded, saying to himself: there were more people here when I retired. What would it have been like to reason with this man or reach him when he had gone inside himself? Dorothee must have known how.

The Sankt Hedwig was also having its effect. Night had shrunk and softened the room. The chandelier light could cope with anything, and Dorothee's pyjama silk was greedy for it. Ute wanted to tell her how beautiful she looked, and how she wished she could dress like that. But Mama, if she'd heard, would probably have said something mean. She would have compared the pyjamas to Julius's.

—What line of work are you in these days? Mama said.

—Let's consider our ages, shall we?

Mama sat upright and beckoned a waiter carrying goose and potatoes.

—There are dumplings, too, Dorothee said. If you'd like some. We're most proud of them. White pepper is so often forgotten about by modern cooks.

—I'm sure mine are better, Mama said.

—I've never been one for criticising something I haven't tried.

Mama tried the dumpling and wordlessly gave them her approval. Instructions were given to the waiter to bring more. As hungry as a gull and in the mood to take everything that was on offer, she hummed to herself as she picked the meat off a goose leg whose bones, with no discernible awareness that they were not at home, she placed on the tablecloth.

It pleased Ute to think of Mama as this woman's equal. And, that night, it hurt with an echo of the ache she had once felt for Dorothee, to think of how much she loved her mother. In the same posture as she was now adopting for her haircut, Ute tucked her chin into her chest while Dorothee discussed the Sankt Hedwig.

—It needs freshening up. I'd like to clear it out and start again. But Felix won't hear of it.

—Julius loves your good taste, Mama said.

—You don't have to be so kind.

—He has a weakness for any sort of kindness, as you know.

—Ute? Dorothee said. Once today is out of the way, we would like to invite you to lunch at the Sankt Hedwig every week. You and family, friends, friends of friends, whatever you like. We will be there every Sunday at noon, but please arrive whenever you like. We would like to host you and to see how we can help you in your life.

But something was wrong with Papa. Something was wrong with Mama. Only now did Ute remember that Dorothee's hands had been trembling.

—Let's call it a night, Mama said.

Dorothee kept on. —I would like to help you, she said.

Mama cocked her ear as if she had been listening carefully. She was eating roast potatoes with her hand. Her cheeks plump with red cabbage, her chin shining with grease. But her expression was different from anything Ute had seen before. And Dorothee, accustomed to a more receptive audience, looked completely lost. Her gifts having deserted her, she picked at the tablecloth. Her arthritis seemed quite pronounced as she returned the picked-off goose leg to Mama's plate. Not only did she want everything cleared, she wanted everyone gone.

Ute couldn't help but feel differently about her than she had. She had—then—been embarrassed for Dorothee, for being so upbeat on an occasion that just hadn't called for it.

Mama had been determined to take as much time as she needed to shear the hair as short as she could. She knew Ute's head by heart. Her breath warm on a neck that had not been bare in so long.

She could have said anything she wanted to, but Mama said, —I didn't have a choice in the matter, and nor do you.

—Meaning?

—Meaning Papa found someone with real warmth in her soul, more than I ever had in mine. It wasn't even what he was looking for. He would have been happy with what he got on the surface. It was his awful fate to have an affair with a woman who was actually worth falling in love with. She left for Scotland overnight, without saying goodbye. There was a limit to my sympathies for this woman, as you can imagine, but I hadn't bargained on your father stepping into a lake of—he started to drown in his own sadness. I have never seen anything like that. I've certainly never felt grief like that. Not for my parents. He was unhoused. Do you know what that means?

—I can imagine, Ute said.

—Do imagine it, Mama said. Imagine your father when she left. This was when he was well, so imagine him unable to speak, or to go to work because he would have sliced himself in two with a piece of glass. He was incapable more or less overnight. I hated myself for all of it. But that was just good common sense, I can see now. I had to pretend I was angry with him when I wasn't. I felt sad for him to have lost that person who made him feel that way. And I was happy for him, in another way, that he got to experience a love that I couldn't provide. I enjoyed the fact that I could see it if he couldn't. He loved her with all his heart. Something left him when she went away. But I couldn't put it back. I hadn't put it there in the first place.

When Ute turned around, Mama's eyes were glittering.

—Do you understand me now? she said. She slid the clippers across the table.

A silence followed—filled with all their old helplessness—and it grew deeper still, Mama was holding onto it, until a voice came suddenly and in a blur.

Ute ran outside without a thought.

Whether Papa knew it or not, he was alive. There he was, arm in arm with Seanie as if returning from a date. One of them, at least, had gotten lucky.

For all Ute knew, Papa could have spent the entire night floating in the sky, tearing out his heart and throwing it in the Neckar, and no more was going to be said about it.

He was being very indecisive in his movements. He was holding a plastic beaker of water and he had torn his trousers and lost his shirt but no one was in any hurry to get him anything new to wear. Mama saw to it that he got hoisted inside.

—What did you do to yourself, Julius?

Mama bent her head to hear that Papa was saying he had had enough for one day. She guided him towards the bedroom.

—Very sensible, Julius, Seanie called out. Up the wooden hill to Bedfordshire. We've knocked enough craic out of it for one night.

It was as if Seanie was having to be heard over farm machinery.

—Did someone plough into you? he said.

—Perhaps they did.

—Was there a lawnmower involved?

—Is it that bad? Mama did it.

—She'll get the hang of it. But it's nice, we can see your face.

She took his hand—oh there was no need to be such a silly crybaby about it—and led him to the table and the seat that Mama had just vacated. All the eggshells made it seem as though he had just finished breakfast in a guesthouse.

Julius wouldn't be in need of any company today, so Seanie was thinking of a day off. After their bit of breakfast, they might go for a walk by the river, or they could go up to the vineyard, there was no need to hurry, they could take their time. He was thinking about what was left of the growing season, the grapes' need for the warmth of the sun to help them ripen, and that he was sorry for all the rain this past week, he'd see what he could do about the storms, he'd have a word.

Apart from all that, they hadn't had a summer like it in years.

The thought seemed to invite a kiss. And she didn't know what amused her more, the unexpected moment of decisiveness or that the idea came to her when it did. Otherwise, it may not have happened at all. Then she was careful to take a seat opposite him, but not in recalling their afternoon on the river—only a day or so ago? They could at this moment do the very same thing, jump, but landing where? In water, on cobbles, or in a bedroom's dawn gold?

—Would you be committing a crime if you changed out of that suit? she said.

—I don't want to blow its trumpet, but it might walk away by itself.

—I'll find something of Papa's for you.

—You should have seen him, Seanie said. Young Julius out in all weathers.